Gifted

Gifted

Beth Evangelista

Walker & Company

New York

First published in the United States of America in 2005 by Walker Publishing Company, Inc.
Distributed to the trade by Holtzbrinck Publishers

For information about permission to reproduce selections from this book, write to Permissions, Walker & Company, 104 Fifth Avenue, New York, New York 10011

Library of Congress Cataloging-in-Publication Data

Evangelista, Beth.
Gifted / Beth Evangelista.
p. cm.
Summary: Arrogant, mentally gifted George Clark has dreaded the eighth-grade class camping trip and its inevitable bullying, but a hurricane and a friend's loyalty make him realize what is important in life.
ISBN 0-8027-8994-3 (hardcover)
[1. Gifted children—Fiction. 2. Camping—Fiction. 3. Bullying—Fiction. 4. Best friends—Fiction. 5. Friendship—Fiction. 6. Teachers—Fiction. 7. Self-perception—Fiction.] I. Title.

PZ7.E87363Gi 2005
[Fic]—dc22
2004061166
ISBN-13 978-0-8027-8994-5 (hardcover)

Book design by Ellen Cipriano
Book composition by Coghill Composition Company

Visit Walker & Company's Web site at www.walkeryoungreaders.com

Printed in the United States of America

2 4 6 8 10 9 7 5 3 1

For my gifted sons:
Michael, Matthew, and Nicholas.
—B. E.

Gifted

ANITA THINKS THE STORY SHOULD BEGIN WITH the two of us sitting side by side on the steps in front of the main entrance, grimly watching our happy classmates pull into the school parking lot with all their gear, and waiting with hearts of lead for that dreadful moment when we would board the buses. Buses that would transport the eighth grade not only to the camp at Cape Rose but to the terrors that would befall us there.

Anita's always had a flair for the dramatic.

I disagree. Nevertheless, since she's the novelist and I'm just the highly celebrated hometown hero struggling to get his homework done in between daily house calls from Roger-the-Sadist, the traveling physical therapist with hands of steel, I told her to go ahead and start it any way she wanted.

But, "No," she said, "it's *your* story, George," and insisted that I write it because it would be good for me and because I have lots of free time now, with nothing better to do. And I'm to be completely honest, even if it happens to be about her and it happens to be personal. I'm not so sure about this last point, but according to Anita, nothing will ever break up our friendship again. *Nothing.*

I guess we shall see.

1

AS FAR AS I'M CONCERNED, THE CLASS TRIP, or I should say my trying to get out of going on the class trip, actually started the night before we left, Sunday, the fifth day of October. I was in the privacy of my bedroom, having just drunk a twelve-ounce glass of cold water blended with a half cup of Gulden's Spicy Brown Mustard over crushed ice, and I was sitting on my bed, waiting for something to happen.

Just sitting and waiting, and waiting and sitting, with an eye on the clock, watching the minutes slowly creep by. And except for feeling totally bloated and having breath that reeked, nothing was happening. Not a thing. I didn't even feel a burp coming on. I wondered then, not in a panic yet but getting close, if I should have used another type of mustard, something a little more "fast-acting." Because if this Anita-tested method didn't work, I would have to find another way to make myself violently sick—and fast. *Otherwise,* I thought, *by this time tomorrow, I'll be dead!* I'll admit this sounds crazy now, but at the time I was serious, and if you had walked in my shoes for a whole week, believe me, you wouldn't have wanted to.

I guess I should explain that I am the one and only child of elderly parents, my mother having been forty-six and my father forty-seven when I was born, and if you'd ever heard them talk about me, you'd have sworn I was some kind of a model child. And you would have been right, but it was mainly because I didn't have a life, not because I was afraid of my dad. But all the other kids were, and that's what kept me alive.

Now, at the time that I was sitting and sipping my mustard frappé and not panicking, I was exactly five feet short and would have weighed a whopping eighty-six pounds soaking wet had I ever bothered to weigh myself like that, with my brain accounting for at least thirty percent of my gross weight. The rest of me, a lithe skeleton encasing a bunch of internal organs, all packed neatly in a clear ivory skin that got a little dry and flaky when I forgot to moisturize, was what some would describe as delicate. And when they did, it annoyed me. My hair was sort of nondescript, that shade in between blond and brown known as dishwater, but at least I didn't wear glasses, which was one less geek item for Them to razz me about. My big thirteenth-birthday gift was a set of high-powered soft contacts. They made my eyes red all the time, like a couple of bright red beacons, but becoming the butt of fewer jokes made them definitely worth it.

My parents, for reasons that were entirely selfish, named me George Robert Clark after my dad's lifelong idol, Dr. George Robert Stibitz, the Father of Complex Computers, which is what I think did it. Cursed me, I mean, causing whatever growth hormones I may have been born with to grow my brain instead of my body. I'm an M. G. I've been in the Mentally Gifted Accelerated Program since the first grade, and I've won every math and science award for my grade level ever to be offered by the Commonwealth of Pennsylvania.

One side effect of being gifted, I found, was that my teachers absolutely worshiped me. You might even say I had them wrapped around my little finger and that at my lightest word they would have turned somersaults for me—all because I was their Golden Boy. It was *not* because my dad was their boss. They genuinely thought I was wonderful. Really.

Okay, maybe not Mr. Zimmerman, my music teacher. I should say my "incredibly stuck-up music teacher," who hated me as much as I hated him. If you think "hate" might be too strong a word, think again. I *hated* him. Not because he was a short, fat man with a revolting mustache that looked like a coffee stain on his upper lip. And not because, with the exception of a crescent moon of jet black hair, he was gleamingly bald. And not because he had a bleating tenor voice that punctured the eardrums and offended the finer feelings of macho men everywhere. Because I'm nothing if not tolerant of those less fortunate than I. No, the reason I hated him was because he thought he was better than everyone else, including *me*, and it galled me. Galled me to my very depths.

Mr. Zimmerman had been the professor of musical theater at some real snazzy New York performing arts school up until they decided to downsize, "trim the fat" you might say, and it surprised no one that Mr. Z's ample figure was the first to go. Now the Music Man acted as if he'd come down in the world, working in a public middle school in Pennsylvania, and it was his policy to be as snotty as possible to everyone he encountered. Particularly snotty to me. I guess I must have brought out the best in him.

I used to wonder if my dad had hired him out of pity. Then I remembered my dad never pitied anyone in his life. He's not what you'd call a "pitying" man.

Not that he's a bad guy, my father. He just tries to come off that way, like he's big and bad and intimidating. He even let his beard grow just to enhance the fear factor. His face is naturally reddish, and it turns a deep maroon whenever he yells, which is quite often. His eyes are the color of ice, and his hair and facial fur are a blend of iron gray and snowy white. He looks exactly like a wolf. He stands six foot three in his socks, and all in all, he's a pretty imposing figure. He makes stupid jokes that everyone laughs at simply because they *have* to, though he's really quite smart. He taught advanced calculus at the high school for decades until the day came when he decided he needed a bigger outlet for all his pent-up hostilities. And since he preferred venting them on those smaller and weaker than himself, he naturally became our school principal, and Conrad T. Parks Middle School has never been the same.

But it worked out well for me because, like I said, without my dad watching Them and spying out all Their evil ways and putting the fear of the detention room into Their hearts, I'd have been dead already. Head-Bashed-In Roadkill. Which is why I had to start throwing up soon. My dad wasn't coming with us to Cape Rose. I would be totally on my own with Them. And I couldn't throw up only once; what I was going for was the kind of repeat fully automatic vomiting that spells *s-t-o-m-a-c-h f-l-u* to even the most feebleminded of mothers. *My own.*

Actually, my mother wasn't feebleminded at all; she only behaved that way. Back in the days before I was born, she was considered to be a very smart person, and as a parent, she wasn't all that bad. Other than making my bed, cleaning my room, and keeping me in April-fresh-smelling laundry, she honored the Keep Out sign on my door, which is a rarity among mothers these days. Not that I had anything to hide in there really. Other than the files in my computer, which she couldn't access anyway, the only things of value to me were my books and the collection of photographs I had taped inside my closet door. Nothing *naked* there, of course, just pictures that gave me inspiration—and that made Anita see red whenever she happened to see them.

When I thought of Anita, I thought, *If this doesn't work tonight, I'm going to THROTTLE her.* It was her master plan, the secret mustard-in-water formula, and it was supposedly foolproof. It had gotten her out of summer bible camp for two consecutive seasons, but I guessed my stomach was a lot stronger than hers was, even though I fed it less.

Anita New-Face. That's what They called her, but her name's really Anita Newell. They christened her New-Face in the sixth grade. Anita New-Face from the Planet Pimple. She pretended not to hear that. She had bigger problems to worry about. She was finally filling out, only she was putting on fat in places that didn't look good. But . . . she was my very best friend in the whole world, though I never understood how that happened. We had little in common, except maybe a talent for getting out of things we didn't want to do. We'd both been practicing that for ages.

Which is why I was surprised I wasn't spewing like a

geyser yet. And then it hit me. *I'll bet she set me up!* She didn't want to go on the trip without me! But then, her life wasn't in danger. Sure, people were mean to her, but she never got death threats!

Ever since we began preparing for the trip to Cape Rose, I would hear Them in the halls: "We're gonna kill Georgette!" and "Georgette only has two weeks to live. Think we should tell her?" and other equally original crap like that. Never directed *at* me, of course, because that would have constituted harassment, which is punishable by suspension or expulsion, depending on my dad's temper. No, They said these things behind my back. Like in the lunch line. If I didn't maintain a careful, paranoid vigilance, a fist would come out of nowhere and smack the tray right out of my hands *from behind my back*. Guerrilla warfare. Inspired by jealousy, no doubt, though why They had to inflict pain in order to express Their inferiority was a mystery to me. It made me wonder how Gregor Mendel made it through school alive. He probably would have told me, "I know just how you feel," had he not been dead. Textbooks leave out so much.

But if I survived middle school and then made it all the way through high school in one piece, I had big plans for myself. I'd go to Yale to study genetics or, more specifically, cytogenetics, then become a research scientist. I'd discover a way to reverse the damage that DNA had done to my body *and make buckets of cash*. And then George R. Clark, PhD, would show up at his first class reunion in a Lamborghini and not even get out of the car, just pull up and give everybody the finger, then zoom off, straight back to his mansion.

But none of that would happen if my life was cut short

at Cape Rose, and since Anita had failed me, I decided I had better come up with Plan B.

I looked at my camp itinerary. Beachcombing and Seashore Study looked harmless enough. There would be safety in numbers. Orienteering, as well, unless They got me cornered somehow. But it seemed to me that if They were smart (not that They were, but They did have a sort of animal cunning) They'd kill me during Free Time. Or else They'd ambush me at the Scavenger Hunt, Tuesday night's special activity. From what I'd gathered, the Scavenger Hunt would take place in the woods that surrounded the camp on three sides, the Delaware Bay making up side four. Students would be sent roaming about in the darkness, armed with nothing but a flashlight, an empty grocery bag, and an itemized list of all the lame forest materials the science teachers could come up with.

I pictured it . . . me tripping through the woods in the dead of night, my flashlight cutting out on me after I'd dropped it falling over tree roots, being chased by all those dumb jerks who hated me and wanted to see what my guts looked like, as well as additional miscellaneous dumb jerks who didn't hate me but wanted to join in for fun.

My stomach was churning. *Good.* Pleasant waves of nausea were coursing through my insides. I stretched out on my bed in an attitude of agony and switched off my bedside light. With any luck, in a matter of minutes I would be suffering the tortures of the damned. I closed my eyes in order to concentrate, to think positively.

I am getting sick. I am getting sick. I am getting very, very sick.

My stomach rumbled as I yawned the words. I nestled peacefully into my pillow, knowing that I was mere minutes away from spouting like a fountain. Because I was getting sick . . . getting very sick.

Getting very, very sick.

And wouldn't you know, mere minutes later (well, that's how it *felt*) I bolted upright in bed like a jack-in-the-box, electrified. Dawn's early light seemed to be trickling through my miniblinds. I grabbed my alarm clock. It was seven in the morning! I was going to camp! Instead of heaving, I had fallen asleep!

And now I was going to camp!

2

"UP AND AT 'EM, GEORGE! BIG DAY TODAY!" MY father's lupine head came poking in through my doorway, his hearty voice shattering my thoughts like a lit stick of dynamite. "Rise and shine! Can't keep happy campers waiting!"

I whimpered, still clutching my clock, and braced myself for his next line. That slogan of wisdom he liked to greet me with in the mornings: "Today, George, is the first day of the rest of your life!" My dad, forever pointing out the obvious to me.

But he didn't say it. Instead, his head vanished and I heard whistling down the hall. I stared, astonished. Even my dad knew instinctively that those words would have been in the poorest possible taste today, not to mention a total lie. Because if the day held a promise for me at all, it promised to be one thing and one thing only. The very last day of the rest of my life.

"I don't get it," I said to my dad as we drove to school.

"What don't you get?" he asked, not looking at me.

"I'm not getting a grade for this, so why do I have to do it? I'm not part of the regular academic program."

We stopped at a red light, and my dad turned to growl at me.

"Don't tell me you're getting nervous. You've got nothing to be nervous about."

"I'm not nervous," I chuckled. "It's just that I don't see the point of going away for five days just to study the ecosystem of the mid-Atlantic coast. I'll bet I know more about it than the teachers do."

My dad bared his teeth, the closest he ever got to a human smile. "You probably do, George, and they'll need you to help them this week. But it's more than just a science trip. We put it into the curriculum because at your age . . ." Here he broke off and started again. "Did you know there are kids your age, George, who have never been away from home before?"

Obviously, I thought, *he means me and Anita.* Nobody else would have divulged that kind of personal information to my dad.

"Try thinking of it as a growing up experience that no eighth-grader should miss. Not even you."

Well, there was nothing I could say to that, so I said nothing. We pulled into the school parking lot, eased into his designated space, and as I opened the door my father thumped me on the leg.

"This is how you make new friends, how you bond with people. It comes from spending time with them and getting to know them. *And* by letting them get to know you. That's how it works, George. It's not something you can do by yourself in your bedroom, and it's not something you can do by spending all of your time with Anita."

Here it comes, I thought. I had heard it all before. He

had nothing against Anita. He just wanted me to have more friends—"more" as opposed to "one." And I agreed with him implicitly, only I'd found it kind of hard to make friends with people who wanted to beat me up. He had no idea how hard it was being me.

But instead of the lecture, he opened the trunk and dug out my luggage.

"Mark my words, George. When I see you again on Friday, you will not be the same boy who left. And who knows? Even *you* might learn a thing or two."

3

IT WAS ONE MINUTE AFTER EIGHT ON MONDAY, October the sixth. I kept checking the clock on the side of our school building every minute or so with the bubbly enthusiasm of a condemned prisoner. My fate was sealed, and the minutes were advancing too quickly.

I'd accidentally left my wristwatch at home, my Timex Datalink that not only kept track of my important hypothetical appointments but was programmed to sound any of five different alarms in case I found myself under attack, and I would miss it sorely. Plus my wrist felt nude.

The sun had been up for fifty-nine minutes, but the air was still cool and wet, so I had on my prized black aviator jacket that I'd bought at the Smithsonian gift shop on our last field trip. It had a big fuzzy collar that would have looked perfect with flight goggles, but what made me buy it was the fact that it had four secret pockets underneath the detachable lining, and you could never tell when four secret pockets might come in handy. At the moment they contained a five-days' supply of Hershey chocolate bars to keep the blood sugar up to speed. My shorts, however, had been a mistake. They were that Girl Scout green color that made my pale legs look kind of sickly out in the daylight. I pulled my socks up all the way so that only my knees would look sickly. And I was wearing my thick, black-framed glasses instead of my contacts for practical reasons. Not my idea, of course, but as Mother pointed out, a single grain of sand beneath a contact lens spells only one thing: *d-i-s-c-o-m-f-o-r-t*.

In the circular drive where they dropped kids off on normal school days, the buses were ready to roll. But these weren't the regular yellow school buses. They were "coach" buses. Apparently we were to ride in style to the death camp. If you've never heard of it before, Cape Rose had been a U.S. Army coastal fort during World War II, and one thing I'd heard they let you do is go up into the observation tower and pretend you're scoping out Nazi submarines trying to infiltrate our beaches. No kidding! I had never done that before, and I felt reasonably sure I never would. Cape Rose was now a Delaware state park, but the old cement army barracks were still there and were going to serve as our "luxurious" accommodations.

The parking lot was teeming with eighth-graders staggering under the weight of duffel bags. I was sitting on the steps to the main entrance watching my father orchestrate the Loading of the Gear into the cargo holds of the buses. *Seems to be going pretty smoothly,* I thought. *Hope nobody packed anything breakable*. I had no idea what my mother had packed for me, but in the backpack that I would keep with me at all times, I had the necessities of life: my favorite book, my CD player, the rest of the Gulden's mustard in case I became desperate, and my swimsuit. Not that I planned on swimming or anything. I wasn't any good at it, and besides, it wasn't on my itinerary. It was because I'd heard that the boys' shower was a communal one, and if there was one thing I'd learned in this life of mine, it was that a little ridicule went an awfully long way.

"What are you doing here?" Anita asked with feigned surprise, sitting down rather heavily on the step next to me. Her face, I noticed, was especially rosy, like she'd been picking at it. She did that whenever she was worried. (And considering what we were in for, who could have blamed her?) She had on *her* black aviator jacket, the same as mine only a few sizes roomier, and her wiry brown hair was pulled back smooth off her face. It was plastered down with some species of hair gel in an effort to control it, although the strands at her hairline had escaped and were already starting to frizz.

"I thought you'd be home sick."

"Yeah, I *bet* you did," I said, fixing her with a frosty stare, as frosty as I could manage this early in the morning, but she missed it as she leaned over to pick up the papers that had slipped out of her hand.

"Well, I'm glad you changed your mind," she said happily. "I got our cabin assignments!" She held up a paper entitled "Boys," which I grabbed from her, then ran my finger down the page until I hit "Clark, George."

Death, despair, and destruction! I would have been better off not knowing.

Don't ask how our worthy secretarial pool made up lists of this kind, but it sure wasn't alphabetically. Obviously, someone in the school office hated me, too. Ten boys were listed under "Cabin F," one being yours truly and four being relatively benign characters. The other five, namely Sam Toselli, Jason Barton, Gabriel Arno, Drew

Lewis, and Tim Simpson, weren't the least bit benign. In fact, one could only have described Them as demons from hell. I looked over at Them huddled around the flagpole. The Bruise Brothers. Five apes in captivity. Guerrillas with buzz cuts, standing around in royal blue team jackets and dark sunglasses. Probably grunting at one another.

They were the bane of my existence . . . football's biggest eyesores . . . and beginning today . . . my new roommates.

4

I CAN REMEMBER WHEN MR. CARUSO, OUR MISguided gym teacher, wanted *me* to join the football team, I guess laboring under the assumption that having all my bones broken would somehow raise my testosterone level and trigger a growth spurt. Or as Mr. Caruso put it, *grow me up fast.* I never took his advice. I'm fundamentally opposed to any sport that gives people who hate your guts permission to hit you. I suppose it's a survival instinct.

Anyway, They must have felt my eyes on Them because all of a sudden They stopped talking and turned in unison to look at me. I turned, too, farther than I had to, so that I was now looking over Anita's shoulder, and said, "So. Tell me. Who's in your cabin?"

Anita rattled off the names. "Monica-Gibbons-I-Don't-Know-Her, Suzanne-Holderman-I-Don't-Know-Her, Meredith-Brown-She's-Okay-I-Guess, Claire-Seifert-I-Don't-Know-Her . . ." She continued reading the list in silence, grimacing a little when she got to the end. "Nobody too bad." She wadded up the sheet and stuffed it in her pocket. "Or, at least, only one loser."

"And who might the loser be?" I asked politely, though truthfully I wasn't all that interested. I was watching the Bruise Brothers out of the corner of my eye, looking my way still and talking again. I thought I caught the gist of Their conversation when Drew Lewis pointed at me, and they all laughed.

"Does the name Allison Picone ring any bells with you?"

Allison Picone! Allison Picone and the word *loser* uttered in the same breath? Anita had my attention now, in the form of a bitter glare of indignation. Allison Picone was the only girl I'd ever loved! The collection of photographs inside my closet door were almost entirely of Allison, and they dated all the way back to the second grade. Granted, many of them were taken of her in full costume at assorted Halloween parades, and only I could spot her with the naked eye. But I'd become kind of an expert at it, and one day Allison Picone was going to fall madly in love with me. Right after I'd finished saving her life, of course. I'd worked that out in my mind a hundred different ways.

"If you could see the look on your face!" Anita jabbed me rather hard with her elbow. "I was only kidding! I just wanted to see if you were listening. You seemed sort of engrossed." She looked at the Bruise Brothers. "Don't tell me you got stuck with *them*."

I nodded miserably.

"That's not good, George. They're going to torture you."

I nodded again, even more miserably.

"Well, why didn't you make yourself sick the way I told you to?"

"I *tried* to," I said. "It didn't *work*!"

"Your stomach must be made of steel then. I can't tell you how many times it worked for me."

"Fine," I snapped. "Don't tell me."

We sat there without saying anything for a while, until Anita broke the silence.

"Whatever you do, George, don't fall asleep tonight."

"I *do* plan on falling asleep," I said, "and in my own bed, too, because that's where I plan on being when tonight comes."

And I meant it. The bus ride to Cape Rose would take approximately two hours and fifty-seven minutes, and I was going to devote every single one of those minutes to finding a way out of this mess.

We joined the masses as my father, the Human Bullhorn, assembled all one hundred eighty of us happy campers into six orderly lines and announced that we were now in the capable hands of the eighth-grade faculty ("Heaven help them!") and that we were to obey them as we would him. Then without so much as a fond farewell to me, his only son and heir, he turned around and, I swear to you, *skipped* all the way up the front steps and into the building, as no self-respecting principal should ever do. Probably to go around giving high fives to the secretaries and to tell them to break out the cranberry punch.

And then it happened. The first assault on my person. It happened before the buses were even in motion. I was next in line to board. Anita was in front of me, and I was watching her rather wide posterior advancing rather too closely to my face as she climbed up the steps when suddenly two things happened in rapid succession: I heard the words "Ladies first, Georgette," hissed in my ear, then a foot shot out of nowhere and kicked my legs out from under me. I fell forward, and just as the bottom step of the bus rose quickly to meet my face, an arm shot out from the other side of nowhere and caught me around my chest.

"You okay, George?"

I gaped as my benefactor pulled me to my feet. It was Sam Toselli. Over my head he yelled, "What did you do that for, you idiot?" I turned to look up at Gabriel Arno, a defensive tackle for the football team who'd obviously missed his calling as a kicker. Sam bent down, picked up my backpack, handed it to me, and then made a clumsy pawing gesture on the front of my jacket, as if he were dusting me off, which made me gape again. This was not the same person who, as recently as Friday, had offered to rip my lungs out through my nose and then ram them back down my throat again. This was somebody new. Was the ape evolving?

"Thanks," I told him, still gaping while mounting the steps.

This needed thinking about. Maybe my future wasn't as bleak as I'd thought.

5

I'D LIKE TO SAY THAT DURING THE BUS RIDE TO Cape Rose I came up with Plan B, and that upon our arrival I would be only moments away from spraining my ankle, or knocking a tooth out, or slipping into a coma and being ambulanced home. I'd like to say that, but I can't. I had too much to think about.

Anita and I had a seat sort of in the middle of the bus, and Sam and his henchmen were all the way in the back. Now, ordinarily this proximity would not have prevented Them from heckling me, but They didn't. They didn't utter the faintest peep, which made me think furiously well into the second hour of our trip. It was baffling.

Sort of like the photograph in my closet gallery of Sam Toselli and me with our arms around each other's necks. My mom had snapped the picture back in the fifth grade when the two of us were enjoying a brief friendship. We were cocompetitors for the Pennsylvania Junior Scientist Award, us and about five hundred other fifth-graders statewide, and we spent a lot of time together working on our projects. It boggled the mind to look back on it. Sam had been quite nice then, and actually happy for me when I won first place even though he didn't get so much as an honorable mention. It's funny how things change. When I say "funny," what I mean is "peculiar." I think I kept the picture to remind myself that truth really is stranger than fiction. And now *this*.

Anita spent much of the drive writing like crazy in her journal. I knew she wanted to be a writer one day, but if you'd asked her, she would have told you she didn't like to think about the future. The present was bad enough. At one point curiosity caught me in its grasp and I leaned over her lap to sneak a peek, but all I saw were the words "Anita and George" etched inside the cover of her notebook, each flowery letter in a different colored marker. Anita gasped and slapped the notebook to her chest. I looked away quickly. I was only going to ask why on earth I didn't get top billing, but I let it go. She's so touchy when she's writing.

She must have been writing the sequel to *War and Peace*, nearly filling up an entire spiral notebook with hardly a pause. I divided my time between chewing over recent events with the Bruise Brothers and rereading *A Tale of Two Cities*, my favorite book of the moment, though not really rereading it. More like picking out my favorite chapters and reading them, and avoiding the ending, which I'd always thought was kind of a letdown. What fascinated me about the book was how two characters trade identities, and one of them not only takes on the other guy's punishments but seems to get some sort of kick out of doing it. Pure fiction, I know, but just imagine it! Where could *I* find such a person?

So, what with Anita, the Bruise Brothers, Charles

Dickens, and gazing at the back of Allison Picone's dainty golden head, my time riding the bus to Cape Rose was completely taken up. Before I knew it, we had turned off the main road and onto a gravel drive that snaked through a vast seaside woodland. The drive ended in a parking lot, where the buses proceeded to dump us and hightail it out of there in a swirl of stones, leaving us to trek the eighth of a mile or so over rough terrain through the forest to the campsite on foot.

My first impression of camp, after we'd left the wooded path and emerged into dazzling sunlight, was sand, sand, and nothing but sand. It was ridiculous! I mean there was forest all around it, so why they built the barracks on a sand trap instead of knocking down a few useless trees and building on solid soil was beyond me. I hate sand! When it gets in my hair, it takes weeks to get rid of.

My second impression of camp was how much it reminded me of pictures I'd once seen of Angola State Prison. Only this facility had slightly less charm.

The living quarters consisted of four single-story cement buildings opposite an identical row of structures with about fifty feet in between them, an area labeled "the Compound" on our maps. Each building was separated into two distinct "Cabins," and letters were painted over the doorframes to distinguish which was which. One latrine per sex stood at the end of each row of cabins. Running lengthwise through the Compound and separating the boys' lodging from the girls' was the mess hall, or "Dining Hall," as it was euphemistically called on our maps, and it had a big red banner draped across its roof proclaiming, "Welcome to Cape Rose," just to rub our noses in it. At the very edge of the Compound, against a backdrop of very realistic-looking sand dunes, stood "the

Administrative Office Slash Nurse's Quarters," a newer-looking two-story building. I assumed this was what the faculty of Parks Middle School was using as a place to stash their beer coolers and as a secret hangout.

Our first order of business was to transport our gear to the cabins and then to proceed directly to the "Dining Hall" for orientation and lunch. I trailed the Bruise Brothers at a safe distance and looked behind me to see Anita lumbering beneath her baggage, gazing gloomily at me, probably wondering if she would ever see me alive again. But when I got to Cabin F, none of Them so much as looked my way. My luck was holding out.

Or so I thought.

Eighteen faculty members had been assigned to chaperone this trip, and not once had I considered which of them might be sharing my cabin until my eyes beheld a terrible sight. In the cabin doorway, blocking the sun with his short, spherical frame, stood Mr. Peter Zimmerman, the Music Man. I had to squint to see what he was doing because the sunlight bouncing off his hairless dome made my eyes water. A clipboard hid his face, fortunately, but his bleating voice gave him away. He was taking attendance. And no matter where my name fell in the lineup, I knew that I would be called last.

"Arno . . . Barton . . . Dunfee . . . Lewis . . . Romero . . . Simpson . . . Sussman . . . Toselli . . . Tucker-Vaughn . . ." He looked up and sniffed the air. "Oh," he said, "and, er . . . Clark."

See? No subtlety at all. I shot back with a snappy, "Hear, hear!" just to show that I could be equally annoying. He let the clipboard drop to his side and scowled at me. Then he scowled at the rest of the room.

"My friends," Mr. Z said, kidding himself, "for the

next five days this cabin will be your new home. But you are not to treat it as such. This cabin is going to stay neat as a pin. I repeat, *neat as a pin*. Now say it with me." He held up his hands as if to lead a choir. When nobody chorused "neat as a pin," preferring to snicker instead, Mr. Zimmerman froze us with one of his uglier looks.

"Cabin inspections," he bleated sharply, "will be performed daily, and the rules will be strictly enforced. They are posted on the wall here to my left. We will review them together tonight at bedtime. On the bunk that will be yours, you will find your name along with a packet of study sheets that you will need in order to complete the science course this week. Now it is time for you gentlemen to get organized. At my signal you may commence unpacking. *Quietly*." He pressed his lips together, eyed each of us stonily in turn, and clapped his flabby hands four times.

We all scattered, simpering quietly, in search of our bunks. Our new home was a rectangular room with whitewashed walls and five pairs of bunk beds placed end to end down the long walls, two on one side and three on the other. Smack dab in the middle of the floor stood Mr. Zimmerman's cot. If it hadn't been for the open doorway and the two unbarred windows, I realized that our new home could easily have doubled as a prison cell in one of the less-cushy third-world prisons.

I found my name. It was on a tag hanging from an upper bunk. This presented a problem. It wasn't that I had a fear of heights, although I did. The problem was kind of medical. I had never been one to sleep straight through the night, having always needed to get up at least once or twice to answer a call from nature. So a bottom bunk was going to be a necessity.

I turned around to locate Mr. Z. He was moving his cot out of harm's way toward the opposite wall. Really throwing his back into it. I walked over and stood beside him.

"Mr. Zimmerman," I announced. "I have a problem." He didn't answer me. He didn't even look up. I repeated my statement a little louder, then had to keep on repeating it until he finally gave me his attention. As did everybody else.

"What is it, George?" he asked in a sarcastically patient sort of way. "Can't find your bunk?"

"It's not that I can't find it," I said. "It's that I don't like it." I wished the others would go back to their own business. "You see," I whispered candidly, "I have a terrible fear of heights."

The Music Man gave his bed a fierce final push against the wall and straightened up to look down his nose at me. He loved doing that because I was the only person shorter than he was. "I guarantee, George, that by the end of the week you will have gotten over your fear. You have to face it if you want to overcome it."

"But I don't want to overcome it," I said reasonably. "I want to move to a lower bunk!" If my dad had been there instead of a hundred and ten point nine miles away, the guy would never have argued with me.

A figure came up beside me and put its great big hand on my shoulder. It was Jason Barton. *One of Them.*

"I'm willing to switch with George, Mr. Zimmerman, if it would help." *Jason gave my shoulder a little squeeze.* "I'd rather have the top bunk anyway."

Mr. Z couldn't look down on Jason, since Jason was about a foot taller, so he added a touch of steel to his voice to remind us of who was in charge.

"The beds in every cabin here at camp have been assigned for a reason. Otherwise, everyone would want what he couldn't have. George will stay on the top bunk and Jason will remain on the bottom, and by tonight"—he gave us a smirk—"the two of you will be too tired to care."

Jason shrugged at me, and together we walked back to our beds.

"We'll switch tonight after he falls asleep, if you still want to," he whispered in a conspiratorial way. And then, without any warning at all, he picked up my sleeping roll and hurled it gently to the top bunk, after which he went about his own unpacking.

I stood there with my mouth open. A big day for gaping, I know, but this was giving me the creeps. Ignoring me was fine. I couldn't have asked for anything more. But this sudden kindness of Theirs was beginning to feel sinister.

I couldn't help wondering when the other shoe was going to drop . . . and if I was going to see it in time to duck.

6

THE MESS HALL WAS PACKED BY THE TIME Cabin F got there, but I had no trouble spotting Anita standing alone on the other side of the room waiting for me, clutching a brown paper lunch bag with both hands. My lunch bag, a neon green thermal one, was crammed discreetly in my armpit. Everyone was to have packed his or her lunch in a disposable bag, and you would have thought that the principal's wife could have followed school directives, but apparently not. Anyway, I joined Anita, and together we surveyed the room. It was filled to capacity with cafeteria-style tables and benches. The teachers were all lined up in a row of folding chairs on either side of a portable movie screen, and Mr. Harris, that elderly man of science, was about halfway down the center aisle, tinkering with a film projector.

In spite of the crowd, I knew we'd have no trouble finding seats. We never did. Whenever I sat down at a table, the kids already there would automatically jump up to go squish in at another table. I used to take this personally, but not anymore. Ever since They became famous for torturing me, the other kids did whatever they could to stay out of the line of fire, and I couldn't really blame them. I would have done the same thing.

But today would be different. I could just feel it. So when I noticed there was room at the table *They* occupied, well, call me daring, I nodded to it and led the way.

"George!" Anita whispered, without moving her lips but giving me lots of eye contact. "Are you out of your mind?"

"What did you say?" I asked rather loudly. "I didn't quite catch that."

And it was just as I'd predicted. Nothing adverse happened. And not only that, as we were taking our seats Drew Lewis and Tim Simpson actually slid over to give us more room! Anita's eyes almost popped out of her head.

"Now I've seen everything!" She hissed in my ear. "What in the world is going on?"

I quietly filled her in on recent developments, then settled in comfortably to watch the film *Protecting Our Important Sand Dune System* with the rest of the guys. The movie was entertaining enough. It starred a cartoon hermit crab whose name I failed to catch, the leader of "The Dune Patrol," which turned out to be a collection of equally verbal marine organisms hell-bent on stomping out erosion up and down the Eastern Seaboard. What I was supposed to learn from this I didn't know, except that I wasn't about to go anywhere near the dunes without a serious weapon of some kind. (I even made a joke to this effect, and They all laughed! Anita just sat there in a kind of trance.)

The movie was followed by an overview of the science program given by the two eighth-grade science teachers,

Mr. Larry Harris and Mrs. Marjorie Love, both of whom I knew quite well, having spent so much of my leisure time in the science lab.

Orientation was followed by a hasty lunch, and the hasty lunch was followed by a mass exodus into the sun-drenched Valley of Death, a.k.a. the Compound, where we stood around waiting to be assigned teams.

The way it worked, the eighth grade was divided into ten teams that would rotate through various stations as listed on the itinerary. Luckily for me, Anita was on my team, and even luckier for me, so was Allison Picone. Not that Allison ever talked to me, but at least when she ignored me, I knew it was because she didn't know I was there. It was *not* because she didn't like me. There's a significant difference there.

Anyway, my team was to meet its team leader, Mrs. Bruder, a Language Arts teacher, at the shoreline for a little beachcombing exercise, and conditions for it could not have been more favorable. A surprisingly hot October sun crowned a sheer azure sky. The white sand sparkled on the beach below. I let Anita carry my backpack so that I could take off my jacket and tie the sleeves around my waist, and I found myself whistling a happy tune and feeling not a single care in the whole wide world, except for maybe a vague apprehension that my Hershey bars might not survive the heat.

Anita was puffing along and sweating like crazy, and her red face was getting even redder. The rest of the hair that had been pulled back smooth in the morning had escaped into wisps of brown frizz, and the impression she gave was one of prevailing misery. I relieved her of my backpack and thought, *poor Anita*, though not for the first time.

Last April she and I went together—well, not together, I mean at the same time—to the spring dance at school, and the reason I bring this up is to say that when Anita applies a little elbow grease, she can make herself look very presentable. Remarkably presentable. I couldn't believe just how good she'd looked that night. She'd let her hair go all curly the way nature intended, and her mother had let her for one night only to wear makeup. At first I didn't recognize her, and then when I did, I had this odd feeling that I was looking at the Anita of the Future. And she acted different, too, that night. Very happy and talkative. Not at all her usual self.

She was talkative now, but not very happy. "Paranoid" was more the word. She was puzzling over the Bruise Brothers' new behavior toward me. I submitted the obvious answer.

"Maybe They like me now."

"Oh, come on!" Anita laughed scornfully. "Not in a million years. No, there's something up. You'd better watch your back, George, especially tonight when you go to sleep."

I stiffened. "Is it so unbelievable that They might like me?"

"I'm not saying that. I'm only saying that it's spooky, that's all. I don't trust them. Do you remember how we first met, George?"

"Hmmm . . ." I scratched my chin and thought for a moment. "No, I don't."

"Well, I do! I pulled you out of a garbage can, remember? It was the first day of sixth grade, and Sam and those idiots tried to throw you out during lunch. People were emptying their trays all over you."

I grimaced. I had forgotten that.

"And right after that, Drew Lewis ran your underpants up the flagpole. Those shorts with the dancing lab rats on them? You remember that?"

I waved her silent. "A harmless locker room prank. *That's what guys do*. It's all in the spirit of fun. You obviously don't know how guys have fun."

"All I know is you wept like a baby when you saw everyone standing out there saluting your shorts."

"All of that was before my dad became principal," I reminded her.

"Right! And then they started picking on me!"

"Look," I told her as patiently as I could, "if you want to harbor a grudge, that's your privilege. But it isn't healthy for you. So let's say no more about it."

We continued our walk in a somewhat hostile silence until we reached the scarlet gypsy who was to be our team leader. Red hair, red cheeks, red lips, red nails. The Bruder was what you might call a "vibrant" woman, but I liked her. She nicknamed me her "Little Gumdrop" and relied heavily on my knowledge of literature in the classroom.

She was standing knee-deep in a pile of colorful plastic pails and yoo-hooing at us with both hands as we trickled across the shore in twos and threes, the rings on her fingers spitting sparks into the hot sunshine.

"Here we are!" she cooed, fitting a red sun hat atop her flaming red hair. "Here we come now! I see we have our packets in hand!"

I scanned the group. Nobody special as yet. Except . . . there she was in the center of her gaggle of girlfriends. Allison Picone. A vision in denim. In the flesh! My jaw dropped just as Anita gave me a wicked jab in the ribs with her elbow.

"Did you bring a pen?" she growled.

A pen. I looked at my hands. No, no pen. I hadn't even brought my packet. This wasn't like me.

"Forget it," she muttered. "We'll have to find one later."

"Today, gumdrops, you shall become beachcombers!" Mrs. Bruder's voice rang out. "Detectives of the bay! You are to follow your Beachcomber's Checklist, and you are to look for at least one organism from each group to put into your bucket. I want you to go slowly and look carefully. Don't be afraid to dig, dig, dig. Get messy! And try not to kill the poor little things. We'll let them loose when we're done."

The Bruder let us loose at the water's edge, each with a pail, a shovel, and a small magnifying glass. As I mentioned before, I absolutely detest sand, so I decided right away that if this was going to work, Anita would have to do the spadework and I the identifying.

"You can share my checklist with me, George," Anita said, getting a little pushy, "but you go find us a pen."

I looked around. Kids were moving to and fro in a daze along the beach, not really sure what they were doing, except for Allison Picone and her ugly girlfriends, who were not moving at all, being absorbed in their usual heavy conversation. Well, call me daring a second time, but instead of approaching the teacher to borrow a writing implement, as I might have done, I walked right up to Allison and her ugly friends. The ugly friends parted like the Red Sea at the sight of me. And then I said to Allison in a clear, deeply masculine voice, "May I borrow a pen?"

She looked at me, surprised, but the important thing was she *looked at me*. Then she said, "Yeah, I guess so," and handed me the pen that was in her hand. Handed it *to me*. And then the ugly girlfriends fell in around her again, and their conversation resumed.

Now this might not seem like a lot to you, but I hadn't felt Allison's eyes on me or heard her voice speak to me since the day I fell in love with her at our Valentine's Day party back in the second grade. I remembered it as a sort of Hallmark commercial, complete with music, although the score sometimes changed according to my mood. There I was minding my own business, sitting at my desk and working diligently on weaving a red and white place mat out of construction paper as a gift to bring home to Mother, when I looked up to find Allison Picone standing in front of me with a big stack of envelopes cradled in one arm. Her other arm was reaching for my face, and dangling from its dainty hand was a single envelope. Over the years the memory had become so misty that Allison had turned into the Lady of the Lake and the outstretched limb seemed to be holding the sword Excalibur . . . but time will do that. Anyway, Allison handed me the envelope, on which "George" was spelled without a single vowel, fluted out the word "here" in a delightfully musical voice, and then proceeded to give me a smile that not only melted my heart, it ripped it straight from my body and left it quivering on the ground at her feet. And it had been lying there quivering ever since.

I sighed. The memory might have been a distant one, but that one distant memory had kept me going through a lot of long days.

And I would have sighed again, but Anita chose this precise moment to startle me out of my reverie with a loud clearing-the-throat noise, followed by a harsh "Will you wake up! We need to look for marine worms." So I shoved my happy thoughts aside for the moment, hefted a shovel in one hand and a bright yellow pail in the other, and proceeded to get down to business.

7

ANITA DUG, DUG, DUG, AND GOT MESSY. I DID my part by peering over her shoulder and offering my encouragement, but when I noticed my feet getting wet, I decided to make a suggestion. "That's where we need to go," I said, indicating the jetty, an outcrop of rocks that projected about thirty yards into the surf.

It turned out to be a real hotbed of marine organism activity. All kinds of scummy sea life seemed to be thriving in little puddles between the rocks. I checked our list. Finding sea lettuce wouldn't prove too difficult. We just had to look for anything green and slimy. I doubted the Bruder would know one algae from another.

As far as mollusks went, first among the choices was the naked sea butterfly. A little risqué for eighth grade science, in my opinion, but I would keep a sharp lookout. Being a warm day, one of these uninhibited creatures might start parading about.

Now, sponges, I knew, liked to cling to the undersides of rocks. Anita reached down into a dark crevice and ripped off a couple of portions of sponge to drop into our pails. I checked off Finger Sponge, since she'd used her fingers to get it. I mean, it wasn't as though I was getting a grade for this.

Another mollusk was the snail, and snails would be a whole lot easier to hunt. Anita got down on her knees and prepared to get messy again, and I located a flattish rock nearby, where I could sit, sun myself like a lizard, and get ready to "identify." Below us on the beach I noticed Mrs. Bruder in conference with Allison and Company, and I surmised that the group was being advised to cut the chatter and get busy. Then, to my horror, they all looked up in my direction, and in the next instant the girls were coming straight toward me. The group was headed by Brooke Walters, Allison Picone's best friend and Chief Lieutenant of the Ugly Girlfriend Corps. I was scared witless, but I managed to maintain my cool by turning swiftly on my rock and falling off the edge of it onto a more jagged one.

Anita put her head up and said, "I can't leave you alone for a second, can I?"

I hoisted myself back up and gingerly felt my rear end. Yep, the seat of my shorts had ripped, but luckily for me my jacket was still tied to my waist and it would serve me well.

"Whatever you do," I said to Anita, "just act natural."

"Yes," Anita replied, "it's natural for me to be up to my armpits in crud." Then she said, "Oh, great," when she saw the approaching stampede. "What in the world do *they* want?"

I didn't answer her. Allison Picone, delicate flower that she was, was treading slowly and delicately over the dangerous footing, while the Ugly Ones seemed to be having no trouble whatsoever swarming up the big black boulders. I saw in a flash that this might be a fine opportunity to rush down and offer her a gallant hand, but then realized that, with the way things were going, I could very well have lost my shorts entirely.

"Hi, George!" Brooke Walters caroled, with a nasty gleam in her eye. "We couldn't find the common mollusk . . . but then we noticed *you* sitting here."

I refused to make the connection.

"Mrs. Bruder said that if anyone could help us, *you* could, George," piped Carly Flynn, one of the low-ranking officers.

I silently cursed the Bruder.

"Wow!" Brooke gushed, spying the contents of our buckets. "You guys found lots of stuff!" Anita grabbed the pails and lowered them to the safety of her crater just as Allison Picone's golden head rose like the magnificent morning sun over a nearby boulder . . . and she was in our midst.

Here's where I shine, I thought. I cleared my throat and lowered it an octave. "What have you found so far?" I was looking directly at Allison, of course, but Brooke Walters took it upon herself to answer me.

"We haven't found anything yet. It's hard to know what to look for without any pictures to go by."

"C'mere, George!" Anita hollered from the depths of her grotto. I excused myself and went to see what was worth interrupting me for. She held up a relatively large snail shell, and I was delighted to see a slimy protrusion wriggling at its underside.

"Check it out!" Anita said proudly.

I took it from her. *A live one.* To Anita, I said, "Well done." Then I held it aloft and said, "Ladies, allow me to introduce you to the common mollusk." Anita gave me a ticked-off look. I don't think she'd intended to share her find with the females. They'd never been very kind to her. But I was determined to shine in any way that I could, so I made myself a mental note that if things worked out to my advantage with Allison, I would send Anita a nice basket of fruit.

"This, I believe, is what is commonly known as the moon snail." I seated myself back on my flattish rock, and Allison Picone seated herself right next to me. The Ugly Ones gathered round me as if I were a cauldron.

"How can you tell?" Allison asked me. How could I tell? I couldn't really, but I thought it sounded good. And then I thought, *Boy, her eyes are really blue.*

"Well, if you look at your lunar calendar, you'll find that we are right now in the phase of the full moon, and that's when these little buggers come out." Did I sound cool? It was hard to tell, but at least I had her attention. And then I lost visibility as a big spray of ocean caught me in the face and saturated my glasses. I took them off and rubbed them on the sleeve of my jacket. Allison must have gotten it in the face, too. She was looking at me with rapidly blinking blue eyes.

The poor mucous-secreting thing was trying desperately to pull itself into its shell and no doubt praying like crazy to the big, slimy snail god that we wouldn't develop a sudden craving for escargot.

"The snail's main part is its foot," I said, "but it seems this little guy doesn't want us to see his." Then I got an idea. I took out the pen and hiked my leg up. "This," I announced, "is the typical foot of the moon snail." I drew a diagram on my knee. I had their rapt attention. "The head is actually right inside the foot, and this little gizmo," I continued, turning it into a pretty elaborate drawing, "is its mouth, right below the head. The teeth are razor sharp." These I drew in a zigzag fashion.

I had no idea what I was doing, but it seemed to be going over well. Never in all my life had so many female eyes been focused on my knee.

And then she touched me. *Allison Picone put her index finger right on my knee.*

"You mean all of that is in their foot?"

I could not answer. Her finger was still on my knee. Then somebody broke the spell.

"I wonder how they *do it.*"

I had no idea who said this, but it brought a tittering laugh from the assembled hags. *Typical,* I thought. But since Allison looked at me inquiringly, I tried to explain.

"The snail is actually a hermaphrodite, meaning it has both male and female parts," and to illustrate, I drew what I hoped would resemble a genital orifice on my snail-foot picture. My experience in these matters is pretty limited.

"Ohhh, he means like *Mr. Zimmerman,*" Brooke Walters cried. This was, of course, followed by more tittering laughter.

"Like, as you say, Mr. Zimmerman"—I tried laughing along—"except I doubt Mr. Zimmerman's private parts are in his foot." I didn't like where this was going.

Then Allison leaned right over my leg, and the air temperature rose a good ten or twenty degrees.

"This is so amazing, George. How do you know all this stuff?"

I almost blurted out that I spent a lot of time watching public television but saved myself before it was too late.

"Oh, one picks these things up here and there," I said nonchalantly, and the next thing I knew the two of us were locked in a visual embrace. *A full five-second one*. I stared at her hard with my eyes opened as wide as I could get them for fear I should blink, right up until Mrs. Bruder very rudely unlocked us, yoo-hooing for her team to join her on the beach. The Ugly Ones got up at once and began climbing away.

"Can I keep it?" Allison asked shyly.

"Of course you can!" I handed over the shellfish, wishing it were a large smelly diamond instead. "The good thing about snails is if you lose one, you can be sure that another one will come along any minute!"

"Why, thank you, George!" she said, pronouncing each vowel in my name to perfection as she dropped the creature into her bucket.

When she was out of earshot, my worshipping eyes following every move of her dainty descent, Anita stood up in her crater.

"ANOTHER ONE WILL COME ALONG ANY MINUTE?"

Anita drew a deep breath. I could tell that she was trying to compose herself. It looked as if she were counting to ten.

"George . . . you are the biggest jerk that ever lived. If you ever do that again, I will cram your head in between these rocks and let the seagulls eat you alive."

She climbed down the rocks away from me, in a real

violent manner, then stopped to shoot a glare at me over her shoulder.

"AND THEY CAN SMELL HERSHEY BARS FROM A MILE AWAY."

Ouch, I thought. *Well, that stung.* It seemed that I was going to have to make it up to her. Something on a grand scale was in order. I mulled it over as I climbed down, and as I reached the sand it came to me.

I'd send Anita a really *big* basket of fruit.

8

ON THE ITINERARY THE HOUR FROM TWO o'clock to three o'clock was designated as Free Time. Anita and I staked out a big shady tree, and after making sure it was clear of any unidentified crawling objects, I took off my backpack and we sprawled at its mossy base. I unwrapped a Hershey bar and broke off a little rectangle. My hand, I noticed, smelled distinctly fishy. Now, ordinarily this would have gagged me, but instead it brought back fond memories of my time on the beach with Allison Picone. I would be careful not to wash it for as long as I could. The ink sketch on my knee I would protect as the maharaja would his favorite ruby.

I let out a contented sigh and opened my book. Anita stuck her hand out, palm up, right under my nose. "You know, you really ought to wash your hands," I said. "They're pretty disgusting."

"Give me a candy bar, you jerk," Anita snapped. "God knows I deserve one more than you do."

The point was debatable, but I dug another bar of

chocolate out of my jacket to appease her, and we both assumed our favorite positions, me reading and her writing. Every now and then I sensed her glaring at me through a couple of narrow eye slits and felt sure that I had become the subject of a comparatively nasty piece of literature.

I don't know if you've ever read *A Tale of Two Cities*. It's required reading in ninth grade, but I'd read it for the first time years ago. It takes place during the French Revolution, a fascinating period of history if you happen to be French, but as I said before, what kept me rereading it was how one guy finds another guy who looks just like him, and the other guy steps in and takes the first guy's punishments, and for no very good reason at all, in my opinion.

I was at the chapter where the first guy, Charles, is being drugged in his prison cell by the second guy, Sydney Carton, so that they can make the secret switch and Sydney Carton can sidle off to the guillotine in place of Charles. Talk about a pal. When suddenly, I knew nothing but pain. A football whapped me in my stomach like a cannonball fired at close range. The book flew out of my hands, and as I lay back against the tree, gazing up at the sun-dappled leaves above, preparing to black out, a face thrust itself into my field of vision. It was Sam Toselli.

"I'm sorry," he said kindly. "Did I get you, George?"

"You got me," I told him, coughing a little. He yanked me by the arm to a sitting position as gently as any ape could.

"Is this yours?" he asked. He was referring to my book. Now, on any other given day he would have kicked it for a field goal, but today he picked it up, brushed the cover off with a muscular forearm, and handed it to me.

"Thanks," I said, stunned, dusting off his football in return. He took the ball and trotted off.

"If you want to play with us," he turned and yelled in a very nice way, "just come on out!"

"Maybe later!" I yelled back.

Anita peered around the tree and caught me grinning to myself.

"Hey, Donovan McNabb! Let me know when later gets here so I can have the paramedics standing by."

Well, I wasn't going to dignify *that* remark with a response, so I treated her to my best and nastiest sideways glare and, sitting with the book closed in my lap, gave myself up to a little quiet reflection. *My dad was right! I* am *spending too much of my time with Anita. If I want to make friends, I have to bond with Them. Get to know Them. Let Them get to know me. I can't do that if I spend all of my time with her!*

I stood up, having made a decision. I tied the sleeves of my jacket around my waist a little tighter and picked up my backpack. If I was going to try my hand at football, then I would have to change the shorts. There was no sense in letting people get to know me *too* well.

I felt Anita's eyes on my back as I sauntered off into the bright sunlight toward my cabin. I hadn't said goodbye because I hadn't felt like it, but I turned around to give her my dirtiest smirk, and thought, *Put that in your book. I've got better things to do.*

Changing my shorts into something suitable for the rougher athletics turned out to be a challenge. My mom, in her infinite wisdom, had filled my duffel bag with plenty of casual day wear, but only one pair of gym shorts. They were the official school-endorsed kind that we all had to wear to Phys. Ed. class, basic gray with

Parks Middle School down each leg. I must have been the only kid who'd brought a pair of these beauties with him to camp, and found myself hoping that one day my mother would leave her brain to science so that the mysteries of my life might be revealed.

I wasn't going to be caught dead in those shorts. I put my brain to work, and in an instant I was rummaging through my backpack for my swimming trunks. These said Speedo on the leg, but I solved that. I turned them wrong side out; ripped off the protective netting, so that they were now a solid expanse of navy blue; and pulled my T-shirt way down to cover the label on the back seam that was now flapping about.

I strode into the Compound to find my teammates, but there were no games of any kind taking place. Just a few aimless students wandering around aimlessly, and here and there a cluster of teachers dotting the landscape. I decided the game must have moved itself to the beach.

When I got there, it was easy to spot the Bruise Brothers dead ahead, and They appeared to be having some bone-crunching good fun. No shoes. No helmets or pads. I decided right away that I would *not* be joining Their numbers. After all, I had to protect the eyewear.

I was just retracing my steps up the pathway when I heard the sound of puffing and snorting from behind. It surprised me to find that it was Sam Toselli and not a charging rhino who'd seized my shoulder to spin me around.

"Hey! George!" he panted. "Where you goin'? You need to help us out there."

"I . . . uh . . . think I need more sunblock." *Sunblock? Is that the best I can do?* "I'm beginning to burn," I told him feebly.

"That's good," Sam said. "Girls like that." He led me forcibly toward the playing field, and I wondered if that were true, if girls really did like blisters and peeling skin. Or maybe they just thought it rugged playing fast and loose with melanoma. *Here's my chance to find out,* I thought. Close by on a blanket in the sand sat the Ugly Girlfriends. And right in the middle of the coven sat Allison Picone.

They had come to watch the football game.

9

THE THING ABOUT DISTANCE AND PERSPECTIVE, visually I mean, is that even the biggest things seem kind of small and manageable when you're not up close to them. Take the football "huddle," for instance. The rest of the guys were crouching, so I crouched, too, but after a while I grew tired and straightened up, and They were still bigger than me. I prayed a silent, heartfelt prayer. Not to shine in front of Allison Picone, of course, because that was clearly out of the question. I asked only that if an ambulance needed to be summoned, to please make it an ambulance well stocked with morphine. One had to be practical.

I crouched again and looked at Sam, who was drawing some sort of pattern in the sand with his big meaty finger. I decided to come clean.

"Guys," I said, "before anybody goes and says 'hut,' I think you should know I don't really know how to play this. The rules, I mean. I don't quite get them."

This produced one or two grunts from the circle but actual words from Gabriel Arno.

"All you need to know is, if you get the ball, you run that way." He stabbed the air with a vicious thumb. "Do you get that?"

"I got that!" I said, nodding confidently, thinking, *But I don't want it!* So I sent up another heartfelt prayer. *Please, whatever happens, don't let me get the ball!* Then after a sharp clap, They fled the huddle, leaving my lonely applause as a bit of an afterthought, and the contest was on.

Now, the funny thing about football from the fan's point of view is that you can never really tell what anybody on the field is doing. I mean it's almost impossible to tell who has the ball. Everyone's just sort of prancing around out there in a purposeful athletic way. But I wished I'd been following the play a bit more closely so that I could have steered well clear of the ballcarrier because the next thing I knew, Drew Lewis had caught my attention by screaming "GEORGE," and a moment later I found that I had become the ball's latest recipient. It flew at me like a heat-seeking missile, and it bit deep into the flesh of my underarm.

All I could think was *damn!* And next, all I could think was *run!* because the oversized members of the opposition were making a beeline straight for me. They were rushing me, crowding me, *thirsting for my blood.* So I dodged and I sidestepped. I ducked and I weaved. Then I gritted my teeth and ran like the blazes, and somehow managed to maintain my presence of mind long enough to remember which way to go. I ran in the direction of Allison.

The opposing team must have read my thoughts exactly; They had positioned Themselves between me and the goal line. All I could see were sinewy arms in the foreground, bunching and flexing and preparing to thrash me to pieces. Horrified, I tried to brake early and come to a halt, but my lightning-fast momentum, combined with slippery sand and basic quantum mechanics, made me slide headfirst instead. And I slid that way, horrified, the next few feet, shooting right through the legs of my nearest opponent before I finally came to a stop.

It took a moment to pull my head out of the sand, and another to see that I was sprawled over the goal line, and a third for the opposition to reach me. Four hundred pounds of finely tuned athletic prowess descended in a pile upon my back. My head was pushed into the sand again.

Still I managed to hear whoops and cheers exploding in the field behind me. Noises I had heard from a distance many times in the past, but never before in my honor. I wanted to enjoy them, but I couldn't, even after the excess weight had shed itself from my back. Instead I got up painfully, coughed out some sand, and felt a friendly hand bash me on the back of the skull. My eyewear bounced right off my face.

"Way to go, GEORGE!" Sam howled in my ear. "That's the way to do it, buddy!"

I blinked my thanks at him as Drew Lewis delivered a hard congratulatory slap on my spine.

"Man! You're the greatest! You slid just like a worm!"

I doubled over to pick up my glasses. They were still intact, but it was no easy task straightening myself back up. The football had gone deep into my side. So deep that it was still there. I uncorked it and handed it over to Sam with an arthritic little wave.

"You're going?" he cried. "You can't go, you just got here! We need you!"

The look of dumb pleading in his eyes failed to move me. "Unavoidable, I'm afraid," I wheezed. "I have to keep another appointment." But I promised to "catch Them later," and as I limped off the beach, believe it or not, for the first time in my life I forgot to look over at Allison Picone.

Because the face I was dreaming of now, the face I yearned to see more than any other at this moment in time, was the face of Nurse Marcia Kobb.

And I hoped she would have a whole slew of cold compresses in her icebox.

10

I DON'T KNOW HOW LONG I SPENT IN THE INFIRmary. I must have slept for quite a while because when I woke up, the sun had sunk pretty low over the trees and I was feeling distinctly better, albeit a little stiff. I doubt if Nurse Kobb believed me when I'd explained the cause of my injuries, but to her credit, she'd put on her best cotside manner and packed me in ice with no further questions.

I pulled out my itinerary. My team had been scheduled for Seashore Study from three to four, but I could tell that it was well past four o'clock. *We must be in Clubs* I decided. "Clubs" was something one signed up for, and since I hadn't signed up for anything, I didn't know where that left me. The only thing I could think to do was go to the "Dining Hall," where I felt sure there'd be at least one teacher sneaking a between-meal snack who'd be happy to tell me where to go.

I had scarcely crossed the threshold, however, when I found that some kind of club was meeting there. Twenty to thirty kids were sitting cross-legged on the floor, and Mr. Zimmerman was pacing in front of them, gesticulating with one hand while reading aloud from a paper held in his other hand. *This must be Play Club,* I thought, *or "Zimmerman's Follies,"* as his plays were generally called. This was *not* where I wanted to be. I started backing out of the doorway and was almost free and clear when the waving hand of one of the cross-legged arrested my movement.

"George!" Anita whispered, motioning me to her. I approached reluctantly. "I didn't know where you were. Come sit down."

"I can't," I whispered back. "I have to find my club."

"MR. CLARK! HOW KIND OF YOU TO JOIN US," Mr. Zimmerman's voice echoed around the room, perforating the eardrums. "WON'T YOU HAVE A SEAT? UNLESS YOU'VE GOT SOMETHING YOU'D LIKE TO *SHARE* WITH THE GROUP."

Forty to sixty eyes studied me.

"I don't think I'm supposed to be here," I said, backing away.

He reached for his god-awful clipboard, and I guess he must have found my name because the next thing he said was, "I JUST FOUND YOUR NAME. SO I WOULD SAY THAT *HERE* IS EXACTLY WHERE YOU'RE SUPPOSED TO BE."

"I signed you up," Anita mouthed.

"WHAT!" I mouthed back. I sank to the floor beside her.

"I didn't know what else to do! After Free Time I couldn't find you anywhere, and then you never showed up for Seashore Study. It was either this or Arts and Crafts. You ought to thank me."

"Thanks," I said. "Arts and Crafts" was stupid and should have been called "How To Make Nothing Out of Something," but *this* was deplorable!

"NOW, IF MR. CLARK HAS NO OBJECTION, I'D LIKE TO CONTINUE," the Music Man said, and proceeded to do so.

Having arrived so late, I was completely lost as to what the hell he was talking about, but from the gist of it, I gathered he was getting ready to turn this troupe of teenage no-talents into performers. Performers who would do justice to the short musical play he'd composed with his own fat fingers. The curtain would rise on Zimmerman's Follies on Thursday night, our last night of camp, and instead of being somewhere in the back of the audience hurling tomatoes at the stage, I'd be on it!

I drew my knees up, pressed my forehead against them, and shut my eyes. I think if I could have fit my hands around Anita's neck, I would have choked the life out of her right then and there.

And not a single jury on the planet would have given me anything harsher than its deepest sympathies.

The way it developed, though, things might have been worse. Anita and I left Play Club not with scripts but with stage crew directions. Mr. Z must have had the two of us pegged as *super*-no-talents, and for the first time in my life, I wasn't going to argue with him.

"Where to next?" Anita asked brightly, as if we were still the best of friends. I dug out my itinerary wearily.

"Clubs end at five o'clock," I yawned, "and dinner starts at five fifteen, so I guess we just stand here."

"Why are you mad?" Anita asked softly. I turned away. She gripped my shoulders, pulling me back to face her. "You're mad at me, George. I can tell."

"What makes you think that?" I asked, studying the sky. Truthfully, I wasn't mad at her. I was sick of her.

"Okay," she said, eyeing me stonily. "If that's the way you want it. Go ahead. Be mad, then!" And turning abruptly, with a swift flip of brown frizz in my face, she stomped back into the mess hall.

I felt a little bad then.

Okay, maybe more than a little, but then I was suddenly glad she was gone. The Bruise Brothers were heading my way.

"Look! There's my man," Sam shouted. "It's the Worm!"

The Worm? Not a name I would exactly relish, but one I would accept in a generous spirit. Tim Simpson looped a heavy arm around my neck, then gave my head what I believe is commonly known as a noogie.

"We wondered what happened to you!"

"Yo, what's this?" The stage crew directions were ripped from my hand. "You're in Zimmerman's Follies?" Gabriel Arno chuckled, shaking his massive head. "You're into that? That's for geeks."

"It was an accident," I replied truthfully. "A horrible accident. I don't know how it happened."

"Not to worry, buddy. You'll slide outta that situation, 'cause you're the Worm!" It was Sam who said this, and from the way he said it, it sounded as if what he meant to say was "You dah Man," and all of a sudden I realized that I was one of Them. *They liked me now!* We were friends! I was part of the brotherhood! And even though I still counted myself a little higher up on the food chain (okay, a lot higher up), I thought, *At the rate They seem to be evolving, who knows? They might even catch up to me in a few years!*

So when the time came for us to head in for dinner,

Sam, Jason, Drew, Gabriel, Tim, and I (together as a team) *muscled* our way through the Compound and into the mess hall. And after we'd gotten through the doorway, Sam, Jason, Drew, Gabriel, Tim, and I (once again, acting as a team) *crushed* our way through the crowds and into the dinner line.

At least I think that's what happened. Being trapped in the middle of our team, I couldn't really tell what was happening around me. But I think it's safe to say we did a fair amount of *crushing* and *muscling*.

And all I can tell you is, *Boy, did it feel good!*

11

"HERE," JASON SAID, SHOVING A TRAY INTO my ribs. I craned my neck and smiled up at him.

"By the way, that was very kind of you," I said. "Offering to switch bunks with me this morning."

"We still can if you want," he said. We moved down the line, and he started slopping macaroni and cheese into a big mound on his tray. I watched him, fascinated. The cheese looked like yellow Jell-O and smelled like chemicals, but maybe that's what built muscles. All I had so far was fruit cocktail and a pair of oatmeal cookies. The two safest foods up there, but probably not great for bodybuilding. I hesitated and put a dollop of macaroni and cheese on my tray, then immediately wished I hadn't. The yellow stuff spread right over into the cookie section.

"C'mere if you want to hear something," Jason said. He moved to a table, and I followed him. When we sat down, I noticed Anita sitting alone at another table a couple of rows away, staring down at her food, not looking at me, but it felt like she was. My heart bled for her in that moment, and I wished she could have made more of an effort to mix with other people instead of being such a loner. But I forgot all about her as soon as Jason started speaking.

"Ever play Smear the Queer?"

I shook my head. My eyes must have doubled in size.

"It's a football thing. We play it sometimes just to mess around. See, one of us has the ball, and the guy with the ball has to make it through the line and the rest of us try and take him down. It's fun as hell."

I gave him a weak smile.

"We're gonna play it tonight, only a *different* kind of Smear the Queer," Sam grinned at us from the other side of the table. Gabriel and Drew slapped Their trays down next to his while Tim knocked me aside in a sharp, friendly fashion and placed his meal beside mine.

"And guess who the queer's gonna be?"

They all looked right at me. The alarm I felt must have shown on my face because Sam explained quickly, "It's gonna be Mr. Zimmerman."

I was confused. "I didn't know he was a football enthusiast."

"He's not," Sam said. "So we have to play it with shaving cream. Get it?"

"I get it," I nodded, without the slightest idea what "it" was.

"As soon as he falls asleep . . . he's *ours*."

"Oh!" I said, getting it and feeling my eyes grow again. "Where does one find shaving cream at camp?"

"We brought it with us."

I wondered how They knew the Music Man would be sleeping in Their cabin, but decided They would probably have smeared any unfortunate chaperone They had.

"But won't we get in a lot of trouble?" I asked with a light laugh, trying not to dampen Their spirits. Still, it was an important point and one that I felt should not be overlooked.

"No way," Sam said. "He won't know who did it. He can't punish the whole cabin, and the other guys won't say nothing."

"But what about the empty cans?"

"We'll hide 'em," came the reply, and I could see They'd certainly covered all Their bases. I looked around the room to catch a glimpse of our intended victim, but Mr. Zimmerman was nowhere to be found. He was probably off having his dinner in solitude. At school he always ate by himself in the music room. An *anti*social butterfly. Then I remembered what I had in my backpack.

"Would mustard be helpful? I just happen to have some."

They looked at each other.

"What kind?" Tim asked. I told him. For some reason They eyeballed each other as though conferring. Maybe this was an important technical detail.

"Cool," Sam finally said. "You can use that. Unless," he grinned, "you turn chicken. You're not gonna chicken out on us tonight, are you George?"

"Of course not!" I said, chuckling heartily, a thing I've never seen chickens do. "I do this sort of thing on a frequent basis!" Which made Them laugh, too, like a collection of hyenas, and I noticed the fuller Their mouths were, the harder They laughed. But They were my friends now, so I just looked away.

To my relief, no more was said about the evening's plans, and by the time dinner was over, it was almost dusk. The last two items on the day's agenda were

Movie Time and Monday's Special Activity, a bonfire on the beach. I was hoping that the movie would be something appropriate and inspiring, like *Jaws*. Instead, it turned out to be *The Old Man and the Sea*, killing two birds with one stone for the language arts department, as we just happened to be in the middle of a unit on Ernest Hemingway.

Near the end of the movie, I saw Sam and Jason creep away from Their places on the floor. I wondered what sort of mischief They were up to, but didn't feel confident enough to ask my new best buddy, Gabriel Arno, to clue me in. Gabriel still had an odd way of looking at me, as though he were dying to find out what my vital organs looked like, and I had no desire to show him. He was my friend now, but he was a *scary* friend. It was widely known that Gabriel Arno kept a king snake at home for a pet, and that one day when Larry the King Snake decided, ill-advisedly, to bite his master on the arm, Gabriel Arno countered the attack with a bite of his own, a bite so vicious that the serpent had to be rushed off to the vet for a course of antibiotics. It was *my* policy around Gabriel to always wear a blank look on my face and try never to make eye contact with him, and, of course, to resist biting him on the arm, all of which I did while we watched the movie. By the time Sam and Jason joined us on our walk down to the beach, I had forgotten They'd ever left us in the first place.

The bonfire was blazing away when we got there. I looked past it at the flickering profile of my former friend, Anita, sitting a little way off in the sand, hugging her bent legs and staring out at the dark ocean. I wondered what she was thinking about, then answered my own question. She was thinking about me.

That choked me up a little.

"Anita New-Face," Drew Lewis exclaimed in a carrying voice, looking where I was looking. "She's not your girlfriend still, is she?" I thought I saw Anita stiffen, but it was too hard to tell in the gloom.

I turned around and got right in his face.

"She was *never* my girlfriend!" I said quietly. "And we're not friends anymore." I cast a surreptitious glance over my shoulder, but it was okay. Anita had left.

"Just checking," Drew laughed, and for some reason apparent only to him, he reached down, picked up a handful of sand, and threw it hard into the fire. I guess he liked seeing all the sparks fly out. Or maybe he just liked making the kids in front yelp and jump back. At any rate, he was quite the comedian.

I passed the rest of the evening this way, watching the hilarious high jinks of my new friends, which consisted of pushing, shoving, laughing, spitting, and the occasional wedgie-ing, but somehow I couldn't fully enjoy them. I was preoccupied. Thinking of *her* you see, and it was driving me crazy. I kept searching for that distinctive head of hair among the huddled masses, but it was useless. I saw not a single sign of Allison Picone. A major disappointment. I brooded about it for a long time, until I thought of a bigger problem to replace it.

The shower situation. I was still way too self-conscious to consider baring myself in public, but I knew that parading around the boys' shower in my swimming trunks would look even worse. Luckily, all was solved when I found myself first at the showers, and as the result of some rapid thinking, I saw that all I really needed to do was get my hair wet *fast* and then get the heck out of there, which was what I did, and nobody was the wiser.

Afterward, as we readied for bed, Mr. Zimmerman made good on his threat to read us the Rules of the Cabin, and amazingly enough, not one of us heckled him. I think we'd decided to let the man hang on to whatever little dignity he possessed before the shaving cream would forever foam it away.

And as I climbed up to my bunk to await zero hour, I felt the tension in the air. I have to confess I was more than a little nervous. I sent skyward my last heartfelt prayer of the day, as any soldier might before the ensuing battle. I prayed that the smearing would go off without a hitch of any kind and that none of us would suffer the consequences of his actions.

Particularly not *me*.

12

IT WAS UNNATURALLY QUIET FOR A ROOM FILLED with eighth grade boys, and I was surprised Mr. Z didn't smell a rat, considering that he was bunking with about six of them. It took a while, but eventually high-pitched snores hit the airwaves above his bed, and a minute later I heard the rustle of someone getting out of his bunk followed by the faint sound of a can being shaken. Then a hand tugged my sleeve and Jason Barton's face appeared.

"George," he whispered. "Go ahead."

I went ahead. I climbed down from my bunk with my heart thumping loudly in my chest and a loaded condiment in my hand. A single turn of the no-drip spout and, *click,* the safety was off.

And I have to tell you that once I got started, I just couldn't stop! It was *tremendous.* I was defacing school property, so to speak, and for the first time in my life I could appreciate how the other half lived. I heard a whispered "Go, George, go!" and, thus encouraged, began squirting my Gulden's Spicy Brown Mustard in random designs and concentric circles all over my target, concentrating mainly on the pillow area since my bottle was only half full. And when I stood back to admire my artwork in the faint moonlight, I knew for certain that this act, and this act alone, would forever cement my status as a Bruise Brother. Nothing would ever be the same for me. I had made it! I was on the team!

I was one of Them!

And then the overhead lights came on.

Somebody had flipped the switch, obviously, but I never found out who, because I just stood there staring down at Mr. Z with the empty Gulden's bottle poised in midair. All I could see were swirls of spicy brown mustard on the crisp white sheet and the crisp white pillowcase and the bulging whites of Mr. Z's eyes glaring up at me. There didn't seem to be *any* shaving cream at all, only tons and tons of mustard, way more than I'd had in my bottle. A loud bleat of torment issued from Mr. Z's lips. I looked around; the others appeared to be sleeping.

The Music Man and I remained motionless in our respective positions for what seemed like minutes until he got up to rip the covers from his cot. They were covered in mustard from bow to stern, and as my eyes began watering freely, I suddenly realized where Sam and Jason had snuck off to during the movie, to raid the kitchen for spicy brown mustard!

I stood there like a fool and let him slap the soiled bedding into my arms. I followed him out of the cabin like a fool to the boys' latrine. He spoke not a word to me the entire time, content with making strangled animal cries in the back of his throat. He planted himself behind me at the sink while I rinsed out the sheets, and when I'd finished and followed him to the cabin, I noticed that he was wearing dried mustard on each ear. The rats in the room were still feigning sleep. Mr. Z motioned me with an angry jerk of his thumb to get up to my bunk, and when I'd done so and shuffled into my sleeping bag, he growled directly into my face, "I don't care *whose* son you are! Tomorrow morning . . . *you're mine.*"

I nodded at him, horrified at the concept, and when I heard the springs of his cot groan, I slid my CD player out of my backpack, slipped on the headphones, and shut my eyes. The mysteries of the day had finally unraveled. I had been lulled into a false sense of security. They had set me up, and They had gotten me. They had used my feelings of goodwill and my readiness to forgive and forget past wrongs, *and They had gotten me*. I didn't know what lay ahead of me now. If I were to be sent home for this, my father would have me put into psychiatric treatment, given the nature of the crime, or, at the very least, ground me for the rest of my life. Or, even more ghastly, make me do community service work of some kind. I shuddered. I would have to find a way to get the Music Man to give me a punishment here at camp. No doubt something would occur to me by morning.

And I would find a way to get back at Them. A way so brutally thorough and so thorough in its brutality that it would make Their ugly heads spin. Because as far as I was concerned, this meant only one thing.

This meant war.

13

AT DAWN I AWOKE WITH WHAT SEEMED LIKE the breath of an idea . . . *for revenge*. The radio had given it to me. I'd left my headphones on all night, and the station I'd been listening to kept interrupting its broadcast to give me news bulletins on Tropical Storm Judith, which had stalled off the coast of North Carolina. The people there were being advised to batten down their hatches and start barricading themselves in. For some reason this put the word "bunker" into my brain.

As I mentioned before, way back in its heyday Cape Rose served as a U.S. Army coastal fort, and not only did it have its very own watchtower, it had a bunker, a concrete stronghold submerged within the cape's biggest sand dune. According to the film at orientation, it was located to the left of camp, where the forest met the beach. And the idea I had was really more a visual in my mind. I pictured Them, the five baboons, trapped inside that bunker after I'd locked Them in. Surely a humbling experience, especially after They'd found Themselves prey to every flesh-biting species of vermin the Delaware Bay had to offer. I mean, the bunker stood out there unused year after year. Who knew what might be living in it? The insect possibilities were limitless.

Now, how I would pull this off remained to be seen. I lay quietly on my bunk hoping for another idea to start breathing, and believe it or not, when I opened my eyes, I saw the hideous face of Jason Barton infecting my airspace.

"George, you okay?"

I locked eyes with him and kept my gaze steady, but didn't give him an answer.

"Sorry about last night. We don't know who turned on the lights. We didn't know what to do."

I continued staring at him. Then I decided to play along with his little charade. "What happened to the shaving cream?"

"We bagged that idea. We liked your idea better. Did Zimmerman say what he's gonna do to you yet?"

"Not quite yet."

"Well, hang in there, buddy. I mean, it's not like he can really do anything to Mr. Clark's son, right?" He gave me a nasty little wink before disappearing, and I thought over his parting words.

Buddy? Ha! I no longer liked the sound of that. What did he take me for anyway? Then I got another idea. I would play along with Them. I would pretend to believe Them and thereby draw *Them* into a false sense of security. It would make exacting my revenge a whole lot easier and a whole lot sweeter.

Satisfied with myself, I turned on my side and jumped. The Music Man's face, red with wrath and clashing more than a little with his pink cashmere sweater, was hovering within inches of my own.

"Get up and get dressed," he snarled. "You're in for a very long day."

I hopped out of bed to get dressed as quickly as I could, hoping that swift obedience might soften him up a little, but I was filled with a rock-hard sense of impending doom that made both the hopping and the hoping a little difficult. I noticed the occasional sympathetic glance shot my way by an apelike face, and each time forced myself to answer it with an equally pathetic look of my own rather than let loose the daggers that burned behind my eyes and give the show away. It all hinged on Mr. Zimmerman keeping me here at camp. Then They'd see George at his best. Or worst, depending on how you looked at it.

The Music Man kept me by his side as the boys of Cabin F trooped to the mess hall for breakfast. He pushed me through the line pretty efficiently, and I noticed that our eating habits were not all that dissimilar. We both grabbed a wedge of the same variety of melon and reached for the same species of Frosted Pop-Tart, and we both avoided the more leathery, curdled, and congealed food groups. I found myself hoping that *that* was where our similarities would end. The table he chose was in a far corner of the room and therefore pretty isolated, and instead of sitting on the bench directly opposite me as anyone else would have, the big jerk dropped his tray right next to mine, and I had to slide over quickly before our hips touched. It was like having a conjoined twin. He explained himself by saying, matter-offactly, "If I had to look at your face the whole time, I'd lose my appetite."

A little abrasive, I thought, but I could see the justice of the remark. Having to look at his face would have put me off my feed indefinitely. But after a while I decided to risk it. I had to find out what I was in for before the suspense killed me. So I turned to look at him, and was just wondering how I might broach the subject, when I immediately became mesmerized by watching the man eat. He took the tiniest of bites and then chewed each one about fifty times, and with his skinny mustache twitching up and down as if battery operated, I was suddenly transported back to the fourth grade, peering into the tank of Nippy the Hamster. The resemblance was uncanny, and it took a full minute to shake off the memory and get my mind back on business matters. But eventually I did.

"Are you going to send me home?" I asked, blinking at him engagingly. He didn't look at me.

"You'd like that, wouldn't you?" he sneered. "No, you don't get off that easy, George. You're staying right here with me."

Hallelujah! I thought. "What do I have to do?"

"Hard work," he said, sneering at his melon. "I'll bet you've never done that before, and I've always felt that you were long overdue."

This gave me a sinking feeling, but at least I was staying at camp, which was the main thing.

"You know, George," he said, chewing thoughtfully, "you surprised me last night. I didn't think you had it in you."

"Thanks," I said. It sounded like a compliment.

"You've proved you're pretty good at making a mess.

Now I'm wondering just how good you are at cleaning one up."

I gulped, and a sizable chunk of Frosted Pop-Tart got wedged in my throat. Mr. Zimmerman smacked me on the back sadistically while I choked it down, and I noticed quite a few pairs of curious eyes taking in our little drama.

"Feeling better?" he asked in an insincere way.

I nodded, feeling anything but better. My eyes fell on Anita sitting maybe twenty feet away. She was probably the only one in the room not looking at me, and I wondered how she could have forgotten me so easily.

"Finish up, George," Mr. Zimmerman said, standing up to take his tray back. "Daylight is wasting."

Daylight is hardly wasting, I thought. *It just got started.* But I kept my mouth shut, squared my shoulders, and rose to follow his example. Today I would concentrate on being as humble and contrite as was humanly possible to impress him with the new and improved George R. Clark. Then when the opportunity presented itself, I would find a way to get those apes into that bunker . . .

I looked over at Them, at Their buzzed meatheads and Their phony sympathetic expressions. Sam signaled me with his thumb and forefinger, forming the okay sign, and I did it back to him, thinking, *Okay to you, my fine, hairless friend. Vengeance will soon be mine. Retribution is getting all set to rear its ugly head and make yours* spin.

Then I turned to follow my new life-partner out of the mess hall and into the Compound, little knowing that he was leading me to a fate worse than death.

14

THE GIRLS' LATRINE. MR. ZIMMERMAN KNOCKED on the door, and when nothing but silence answered him, he pulled it open and made it stay that way with a convenient nearby garbage can.

"Why are we stopping here?" I asked.

"We are stopping here because here is where we stay!" he said, not untriumphantly. He walked into the building's murky depths, and I had no choice but to follow. Surely we were breaking a law of some kind, if only a law of nature! But I knew better than to try to appeal to his sense of propriety, since he probably didn't have one, so I continued to keep my mouth shut.

The door led into a little, recessed, alcove sort of room decorated with a counter and a couple of filthy mirrors, but we kept right on walking until we hit the main room, or "center stage," as he called it. There was a shower area at the far end, and in the foreground a dozen sinks stood opposite a dozen stalls.

I saw immediately what my punishment was to be. All

lined up and waiting for me were a pile of rags, a big bucket, and a cardboard box filled with an assortment of toxic cleaning products. Mr. Z held out a pair of latex dishwashing gloves and said, "You can start with the floor over in that corner, George. Oh, and by the way, I'd be careful if I were you. I saw a pretty big spider there earlier this morning." He jumped up to park his can between two of the sinks and sat there looking smug and swinging his crossed legs at me.

He's just trying to irk me, I thought, giving him my iciest stare. I put on the yellow gloves and bent down to examine the contents of the box. Domestic Science was hardly my forte. I decided to wing it and picked up a lethal looking nonaerosol can and made my way over to the corner, where I found out right away that the Music Man had been wrong. It wasn't a pretty big spider residing there, but a whole *community* of pretty big spiders, and they had hair that would have been long enough to braid had I been so inclined. So I did the only thing I could do. I let out a piercing scream.

Mr. Zimmerman burst into an explosion of high-pitched laughter, and if I've described it before as a tenor voice, I can only tell you that soprano was what I'd meant. The noise ricocheted off the tile walls until even the spiders were too shocked to move.

He calmed it down to a controlled simper and dried his eyes. "Let me ask you something, George. What do you want to be when you grow up?"

"A geneticist," I muttered, because it was too hard to mutter "cytogeneticist."

"Ah, George the Geneticist. Do you think a geneticist has to work very hard at what he does?"

"Maybe, but it's hardly this kind of work!"

"But I'll bet it gets messy, the work a geneticist does." He clapped his hands. "Tell you what, George. Why don't you pretend this latrine is your lab and that those spiders over in that corner are waiting to be dissected and studied under your microscope."

"That's high school biology," I told him. "Genetics is a bit more complex, involving cells, and chromosomes, and DNA, and DNA isn't *hairy*." But that only made him laugh harder. The acoustics in the room were insufferable.

"Like I told you before, George, you have to face your fears if you want to overcome them!" he declared pompously.

I bit my lip and began attacking the floor with my rag. What I was trying to accomplish I didn't know. The floor tiles were the color of dirt anyway, so the Music Man would have had no way of knowing whether or not they were getting clean. He just wanted to see me shame myself. And I was doing a pretty good job of it. I was also sweating like a horse. When my efforts had taken me all the way across the room, Mr. Zimmerman suddenly bounded off his perch and stood a moment looking over my shoulder. I sat back, convinced he was going to tell me that enough was enough and that I had learned my lesson, but he didn't. "You missed a spot," he announced smugly, pointing with the toe of his shoe before hopping back up to his seat.

I thought to myself, *If I can find a way to trap the Bruise Brothers inside that bunker, then there's no reason on earth why I can't find a way to get the Music Man in there with Them. And if They're in there long enough, who knows? They may even resort to cannibalism!*

I finished the floor cheerfully then, and when I stood

up to drop my yellow gloves into the box from whence they came, Mr. Zimmerman dropped a bombshell on me.

"If you think you're done, think again. You're about twelve sinks and twelve toilets away from being done."

I don't know how I got through the next hour or so, but visualizing my music teacher being eaten alive by the Bruise Brothers certainly helped. Eventually, though, he must have had an attack of conscience because he told me I could pack it in and remove the gloves. I pulled out my itinerary, thinking the score had been settled and that I was free to move on, but he shook his glossy scalp at me.

"It's not over yet. Pick up the box and follow along."

So I picked up the box grimly and followed him grimly across the Compound to the boys' latrine. Out of the corner of my eye I saw the five Thugs barging up the footpath that led to the beach, and as I watched Mr. Z prop open *that* latrine door with yet another convenient nearby garbage can, I couldn't help smiling to myself. A morning's exertion under the hot sun, combined with so much sea air, would surely leave Them ravenously hungry.

I spent the better part of the morning on my knees in one comfortless position after another, and if there was a lesson to be learned at all from my punishment, it was that latrines are *sick*. Especially the toilets. And to make matters worse, when I straightened up from the one I'd been scouring and released my breath, I found that I was feeling my mom's pain, which made me miss her terribly and wish she could have been there to lend me a hand.

Mr. Zimmerman spent his sojourn in the boys' latrine with his behind stuffed between the sinks as he had done in the girls', only instead of sitting and laughing the entire time, he was doing what looked like paperwork, and seemed pretty engrossed in it, too. *No doubt earning that pittance of a paycheck,* I thought. Still it wouldn't hurt to make nice with the man, so I cleared my throat and said brightly, "How's it going your way, Mr. Z?"

I must have startled him, for he jumped eight inches, and when he landed back on the countertop, I felt the floor quake beneath me.

"Oh, very well! Thank you, George. It's going very well. Yes."

Now I was curious. "What are you doing?" I asked. It turned out to be the right thing to ask because a pleased look lit up his homely features.

"Come over here. I'll show you."

I peeled off the yellow gloves and assumed a look of interest, thinking that if I played my cards right, I could possibly turn this into a lengthy break.

"I'm rewriting one of the songs for the show. You see, when I wrote the musical, I didn't know as much about Cape Rose as I do now. For example, I didn't know that a German submarine had surrendered here. I'm trying to inject more facts into the play. Give the audience a more accurate account of her history without changing the play's general composition, which I still feel is quite good."

I read what he'd written and thought, *He has got to be kidding.* But I put a fascinated look on my face and said, "This is fascinating. How does one learn to compose like this? Did you have to study a lot, or is it just a knack?"

That made him happy. Flushing an unbecoming pink, he said, "A blend of both, I think." The expression he wore was similar to one a dog would wear after being called "a good fella." And a rather simple dog, at that.

"You're not just putting me on now, are you, George?"

He scrutinized my face carefully. "Because if you're really interested in this musical, you can help me with the sets I've got to build. I want them ready for the stage crew before our three o'clock rehearsal."

"Oh, I'm really interested," I said. I really was. Anything that would get me out of the latrine would hold my interest, especially if it involved helping my music teacher make an even bigger ass of himself on opening night. "And I'd especially like to learn something new," I added, to give my sincerity just the right touch. "I was afraid to ask before, but I really want to help you."

"Well, I'll be," Mr. Z said, smiling warmly. He helped me gather up all the cleaning stuff I'd left scattered about, and when he slid the trash can aside so that I could get the box through the doorway without killing myself, I found I had but one regret—that I hadn't developed an interest in musical theater a good two or three hours earlier.

15

SHUFFLING OVER THE COMPOUND UNDER THE weight of my burden, I managed to make eye contact with a group of teachers standing around in a chitchat, and the looks they gave me were looks of concern and dismay. From the Bruder I sensed a certain outrage at what was happening to her poor Little Gumdrop, which made me wonder what the teachers had thought upon hearing *The Tale of the Midnight Mustarding*. What a shock it must have been. I answered their looks with a brave face, one that I hoped would impart the message that "boys will be boys" and that their George could take his punishment right along with the best of 'em, and I followed Mr. Z like a lackey to an area behind the mess hall where large pieces of particleboard stood propped against the building.

"These are the backdrops," he said, taking the box out of my arms, "and what we need to do first is build stands for them. Have you ever built a tree house, George?"

A tree house? I forced a blank look over the appalled one that had distorted my features and shook my head. "But I know how to operate a hammer, if that would help! I remember using one in Wood Shop once."

He stood a moment, lost in thought.

"I have a better idea. How about if you make a trip to my pickup truck to bring back more lumber. Just small scraps. A dozen or so. You can transport them in this . . ." He disappeared around the side of the building and returned pushing an old wheelbarrow.

I stared at him in awe, thinking, *How surprisingly macho!*

"You have a pickup truck?"

"How do you think I got all this wood down here? Go on, George. It's in the parking lot where we first came in. Do you think you can find the way? Or do you want me to come with you?"

"Oh, I know where I'm going," I said confidently, because my agile brain had already grasped the significance of the task at hand. To get to the parking lot one entered the woods, and I realized in a flash that this would enable me to perform a spy mission to find that bunker.

So without further ado I took the splintered handles of the rusty contraption in both hands and set off. Going the distance with this thing would not be easy, what with the ground full of sand and ruts, and, more often than not, sandy ruts. But I wheeled the thing with enthusiasm, thinking not only would I be able to spy out my area of operations but I might also catch an inspiring glimpse of Allison Picone somewhere about.

Navigating over the rut-infested Compound would have been a lot easier had the Compound been less infested with students as well. A number of teams were there now with their team leaders, and divining a course through all that humanity was not easy for one wheeling a barrow.

After I'd made it across and found myself up against yet another team of student scientists, I decided to stop and have a little rest. Because it was *my* team kneeling around at the edge of the forest, and the inspiration I had been thinking about just moments before was right in front of me, inspiring away. And looking pretty industrious about it, too. Allison Picone's yellow tresses were skimming the ground as she bent her head low over what looked like a little pile of dirt. Actually, they were all doing it, bending down low over dirt, even the Ugly Girlfriends, and they were working quietly now, with none of their customary cross talk.

And I could see why. Their leader today was none other than Mrs. Marjorie Love, Science Teacher and Exacting Taskmaster. No one dared goof off in that lady's presence because Mrs. Love, in spite of her name, was nobody's fool.

Anita was there hovering over her dirt, and since I was more than a little curious to know what everyone was doing, I crept up behind her.

You can't sneak up on Anita. I think her wiry hair must serve as an antenna or something because she spat out, "What do you want, George?" while I was still yards away.

I crouched beside her. "What are you doing?" I asked. She was sifting dirt through a little mesh apparatus.

"We're separating the soil from all the other junk so we can test it for non-point-source pollutants, *if you must know!"* she whispered frostily.

Mrs. Love eyed us sharply through her goggles, but seeing that it was me and not just *any* student creating a disturbance, she nodded a greeting my way and went back to her work. I can't say Mrs. Love ever actually fawned over me the way most teachers did, but she always treated me with the kind of respect one scientist would naturally bestow upon another.

Anita was scooping the soil up with her fingers now and spilling it into a little plastic bag, and somehow, without losing a single particle of dirt, she managed to shove her right shoulder back hard so that it almost caught me in my chin. "Will you get lost!" she hissed.

I got up quickly. She was getting physical now. But before I walked away, she whispered, "Is it true you smeared Mr. Zimmerman last night?"

So, word had gotten round. "Yes," I said, "it's true." I figured that if I had to take all the blame for the deed, then I might as well take all the credit, too. Anita just shook her head.

"You know your new friends, George? Well, I think it's a good thing you found them. You guys were made for each other."

She was wrong, of course, but only I knew that. Anita's problem is that she leaps to conclusions all the time and never gives a person a chance to explain himself. I would have told her that They weren't really my friends, that it was all just an evil plot to ruin my life, but I could tell she didn't want to talk to me when she said, "Buzz off and leave me alone!"

I marched over to the stupid wheelbarrow and decided that I would first go to the stupid parking lot and pick up the stupid lumber before I would check out the stupid bunker. But check it out I *would.* Because now more than ever I was determined that Sam Toselli and his brainless band of primates receive the full force of my revenge.

Even if it took me all day.

16

BUT IT DIDN'T TAKE ME ALL DAY. AND LOOKING back at it now, I'd like to tell you that it *had* taken all day and that I'd thought the thing through carefully, and that any holes in the scheme had been sealed watertight, but I can't. Looking back with the clear perspective only time will give, I see that chief among my shortcomings had been a tendency to be a little overimpulsive. And it was partly Anita's fault. What I'd needed right then was a best friend's loyalty, and she'd gone and treated me like dirt. No, come to think of it, she'd treated the dirt a lot better.

I pushed my way along the edge of the campground, en route to the parking lot, and I had the odd sensation of what it must be like to stagger across a lonely desert, finding certain death to one side of you and a life-giving mirage shimmering away on the other. The forest was on my left, a population of loblolly pines, yucca trees, and mixed vegetation growing dense and lush out of the fertile soil; on my right was nothing but parched beach grass and dried-up scratchy-looking bushes that had apparently sprung to life and clawed their way out of the sand. Quite a contrast. But I hardly noticed the weird landscape at all because I was too mad. I turned fuming onto the trail leading into the forest, hardly knowing what I was doing. Anita should have known me better than that! What was the point of having a best friend if the best friend thought the worst of you all the time? There was *no point,* I decided, trudging on, and then I realized that I had no idea where in the hell I was going.

Cape Rose, as the name suggests, is a cape, "an area of land poking into a large body of water," and the terrain of this coastal nightmare was entirely at sea level. There were no hills, no high places I could ascend to pinpoint my location besides the important sand dune system. Navigating by the stars was out, since it was just past midmorning, and in spite of my earlier confidence when I'd told Mr. Z that I knew where I was going, I wished to amend that now and just say I had roughly an approximate idea and that I would probably know the parking lot when I saw it. I cast my mind back to our arrival and could remember nothing except that I'd kept a close and suspicious eye on the Bruise Brothers the whole time and that we'd followed a woodland path of a rustic description. Now I saw that there were several paths of this kind, and they all branched off of the one I was on.

I was debating whether to just pick one or give it up and head back to camp for a compass when I heard a series of twigs snap and the distinct murmur of adolescent voices. I peered into the trees. The twig-snappers turned out to be a group of students, and they looked like they were either collecting samples of plant life or trying to catch poison ivy.

I set the wheelbarrow down and slipped on my black aviator jacket. With my arms sufficiently covered and my legs protected by my sturdy mauve corduroys, I stepped off the trail and set a course through the undergrowth, feeling certain their team leader would be able to point me to the parking lot.

The forest emitted a sweet smell of decay that made my nose run, so I breathed through my mouth, keeping my teeth jammed tightly together so as not to inhale a gnat or something. I passed scattered students along the way, and while nobody said anything to me, I received a goodly number of admiring looks. Mr. Zimmerman had been the least popular teacher in recorded history, and those looks said to me, "George, you rock!" I was an overnight success.

In the near distance stood Mr. Meltz, my Social Studies teacher, talking to assorted kids. To his left I saw an area where the forest petered out, giving way to dune grass rippling in the breeze.

Two thoughts occurred to me at once. If I approached Mr. Meltz for directions to the parking lot, I would receive its coordinates in approximate degrees of longitude and latitude, owing to the fact that Mr. Meltz couldn't answer a question simply. Mainly because he didn't know anything useful. But if I headed left, I might be looking at the very sand dune that housed the bunker of my fantasies.

I decided on the detour and proceeded in that direction, but not without first grabbing a stout walking stick in case I should lose my footing. I strolled straight past the Keep Off Dune Grass sign, bounded down to the beach below, *and there it was.* The concrete face of the bunker, complete with a sturdy-looking steel door. At the top of the door was a small window opening, and at the bottom, reclining against it, were Sam and Jason. They scrambled to Their feet when They saw me, and Jason dropped a glowing ember to the sand, crushing it with his heel.

"Oh!" he said. "It's just the Worm. Why are you here?"

I thought quickly. "Mr. Zimmerman sent me to find a hammer. He said there were lots of tools in there." I pointed at the bunker.

Sam moved to the door and got up on his toes to peer through the opening.

"He's crazy. There's nothing in there but a bunch of old junk. See for yourself."

I joined him, standing up the same way, but I would have needed foot-long toes to get me up that high.

"Slide over," Sam told me, yanking on the metal handle. He pried the heavy door open a couple of inches, then kept pulling with all his might until it opened all the way.

"See? Nothing but junk."

He was right. Dusty boxes and miscellaneous debris were everywhere. It wasn't at all how I'd pictured it. I wanted ancient weapons of mass destruction swarming with spiders and rats and hermit crabs, but it looked just like somebody's basement. It had that moldy basement fragrance, too.

But since beggars can't be choosers and the temptation was too hard to resist, I saw my chance and I took it.

"Hey!" I cried. "What's that over there? Could those be nudie magazines?"

"Where?" they both cried.

"All the way in the back!" I pointed into the gloom. "The very back!"

It worked like a charm. They buzzed inside, knocking each other out of the way, while I, quicker than quicksilver, hurled myself against the door and slammed it shut. My faithful walking stick I jammed sideways through the handle, jiggling it a bit to test its durability. It would hold.

I let out a triumphant "Ha-ha!" as a muscular arm swung out of the window and made a grab for my hair. But thanks to my reduced stature and expert ducking reflexes, I managed to escape unscathed. Then an evil voice growled, "You're dead, Worm," which sent a chill down my spine and me sprinting up the side of the dune. I retraced my steps through the forest at a brisk canter to where I'd left the wheelbarrow, and that's where it hit me. Reality, I mean.

What have I done? When They get out, They're going to kill me!

I steered the wheelbarrow back into camp like a lunatic gardener, and in no time flat, I made it all the way to Mr. Zimmerman's construction site. My chest was heaving. I leaned against the building, trying to catch my breath.

The whole time I'd thought of nothing but sweet revenge, and I cursed myself now for forgetting that after revenge comes *retaliation.* When Sam and Jason got out, my life would be worth less than a plug nickel. I swore under my breath. Then I sensed a couple of bulging eyes on me. I turned around.

"Where's the wood, George?" Mr. Zimmerman had appeared out of nowhere wearing a tool belt of all things. A rather big tool belt. He led me to where a slab of particleboard lay balanced atop two rusty, yellow garbage cans.

"I got lost," I told him, hoping he wouldn't send me back out to have another go at it. There could be no more venturing around camp for me. Not without a great big bodyguard in attendance. I held my breath.

"You were gone so long I thought you'd decided to

chop down a tree or something. Well, we'll let it go for now. It's close to lunchtime."

I released my breath and felt my heart rate return to normal. I would at least have a last meal before being cut down in my prime.

"Take a look at this, George!" Mr. Zimmerman slid the board off the cans. "Can you tell what this is?"

The wood had been cut, and pretty accurately to-scale from what I could tell, in the shape of a World War II submarine. Mr. Z was looking at me brightly, waiting for my answer, altogether too pleased with himself. I studied the thing from all angles, then shook my head slowly.

"Is it a tank?" The fear of death had taken all the sunshine out of my disposition, and I was in no mood to make anyone happy.

"No, no!" he bleated. "It's a submarine!" He came over to join me in my scrutiny of the war vessel. "See the outline of the hull? And the periscope here?"

"Oh, *now* I see," I said in an unconvinced way. "That's a periscope there!" You could almost hear the steam fizzle out of his engine.

"A tank? Does it really look like a tank?" He held his head to one side, doubting his own craftsmanship. Then he shook it. "Well, perhaps the paint will make a difference."

He tossed a package of sandpaper at me, which landed on my toe. "Let's give the edges a good sanding before we break for lunch. We can't have the stage crew getting splinters from it this afternoon."

I took a square out of the package and started doing what he'd started doing, that is rubbing it back and forth along the rough lines of the wood. But not as deliberately as he or as meticulously, because I knew that my ex–best friend would be handling this prop soon, and while a flesh wound and a wound of the spirit were not exactly the same thing, if I could give Anita a wound of *any* kind, then that timeless proverb "What Goeth Around Cometh Around" might hit home to her in a very personal and meaningful way.

Which would, at least, give me *something* to look forward to.

17

I ATE VERY LITTLE FOR LUNCH, WHICH WAS KIND of a shame because the chef had prepared rotini and meat sauce, a personal favorite of mine, and what I managed to chew, I consumed in a moody silence. My sidekick, Mr. Zimmerman, had brought his Follies paperwork to the table, and he was so involved with his writing that he didn't seem to notice my air of despondency no matter how hard I sighed. He'd write something he thought terrific, then make me read it, convinced somehow that I cared. It was all I could do to critique his work honestly, and with his spirits as high as they were, I think my sarcasm was lost on him.

When the man finally broke into song, or rather an obnoxious hum, I turned away from him on the bench and laid my head on the table. I wished now that he had just sent me home. Sure I would have been grounded, but a good grounding sounded kind of peaceful to me now. Just me, alone in my room with nothing but my thoughts and my C drive. No worries. No camp. No Bruise Brothers on the warpath.

Psychiatric treatment didn't sound so bad either. I pictured a kind, grandfatherly, Freud-like doctor "ahem-ing" a lot and telling me mine was an interesting case. I would invent some really good problems. Instead of this. This was slow death!

I peered at the Bruise Brothers' table, its top commanding officers conspicuous in Their absence. The three present seemed happy enough, shoveling in Their food with the same slavering gusto I'd pictured Them devouring Mr. Z with only hours before. I wondered what They thought of Sam's and Jason's absence, then decided probably not much. Thinking wasn't one of Their usual habits.

At this point, the lights in the mess hall began blinking rapidly and the noise died away at once.

"Ladies and gentlemen," Mr. Harris announced, "may I have your attention please." I gave him mine, hoping the old gentleman would explain why he'd felt compelled to wear a dress shirt and bow tie with his blue jeans and hiking boots. It was beyond me. "We have become aware of a serious problem here at camp."

Suddenly, he looked right at me. *They found me out,* I thought. *Sam and Jason got loose and told on me!* Something I was sure They'd never do, since it would stymie Their chances of killing me later. But as Mr. Harris went on, it seemed the problem had nothing to do with me.

"We have just received word from the National Hurricane Center, and it appears . . ." he paused, as if searching for the right words. "It appears that we are right now in the direct path of a category-two hurricane."

Nothing like breaking it to us gently, I thought. There was dead silence, until Mr. Harris cleared his throat.

"Instead of hitting the coastline of North Carolina as was originally forecast, Tropical Storm Judith has made a slight turn and upgraded herself in the process to hurricane status. Now, if she continues on her present course at her present rate of speed . . . Well, ladies and gentlemen"—here Mr. Harris actually chuckled—"needless to say, by tomorrow evening we'll all wish we were someplace else."

An anxious murmur rose from the crowd. Mr. Harris held up his hand.

"So, what does this mean to you, folks? It means that unless Hurricane Judith changes course dramatically over the next few hours, we will evacuate by bus at eight o'clock tomorrow morning, which should give us plenty of time before the storm hits, and—" The lights started blinking again, because a cheer had exploded in the room. He continued much louder. "And that means a change in schedule. We want you to get as much work done in your science packets today as possible. After lunch you are to meet with your team leaders and work until the dinner break. Immediately after dinner we'll have our Scavenger Hunt, and that will be it. Tonight we'll pack our things, and tomorrow morning we'll head for home."

Mr. Zimmerman dropped his pencil onto his paperwork with the dejected look of a man who'd just found out that his ghastly play might never be produced. But *I* was feeling pretty dynamite, having just seen the glorious light at the end of *my* particular tunnel. So I gritted my teeth and placed a consoling hand between his shoulder blades.

"There's no reason why the show can't go on at home,

is there? The auditorium's better anyway. Fewer insects!" I could afford to be generous now.

Mr. Zimmerman brightened immediately and returned the gesture by placing a flabby hand on *my* back. I gritted my teeth again.

"You know something? You're right, George. You're absolutely right. You and I can finish the sets today, and if we do the play at home, who knows? Maybe we could make an even bigger production of it . . . we could add a few more numbers and schedule opening night on Veterans Day. That would work. That would give us a whole month!"

I didn't know what he meant by "us." I thought, *a month from now, I'll be looking back on this as just another bad dream,* but I was content now to let it go. Because if I found a way to stay beside this man until bedtime, managed to stay awake all night, and lived to see the light of day, I knew I'd be able to blow the all-clear whistle until we got home, where my dad would, of course, take matters into his own hands.

The Music Man and I then attacked our meals in a companionable silence, and I was enjoying every mouthful until I happened to look past him out of the window. What I saw there made me choke and sputter. Framed in the glass, looking like a couple of killer apes who'd just spotted the monkey who'd made off with the bananas, were the heads of Sam and Jason. And the looks They gave me were looks of pure venom. Sam raised his hand to make a throat-slitting gesture, and I, to be civil, nodded. I understood completely. I was a dead man. We were clear on this point, and in a sense it was gratifying to know that after all this time, Sam Toselli and I were on the same page.

Even though *I* wouldn't be on it for long.

The heads turned and vanished from the glass only to reappear in the doorway atop a couple of physiques that I hadn't remembered being quite as humongous and brawny as I saw they were now. They were giants really, and as They stood at the head of Their table, no doubt giving Their buddies an update on my life expectancy, I wondered if brains could ever really triumph over brawn.

I felt Mr. Zimmerman's breath on my cheek and turned to look at him looking at me.

"Are they bullying you, George?"

My laugh, meant to sound melancholy, came out as a long, drawn-out fit of croaking.

"What's going on here?" Mr. Z asked, alarmed. "Did they have anything to do with the prank you played last night? Level with me. I want the truth from you, George."

"Well . . ." I said, and I paused. The moment of truth had arrived, and what *kind* of truth I told him would either help me or hinder me. And that, by the way, is what separates us from the apes—the ability to work out a cognitive game plan quick as a wink instead of just standing around making throat-slitting gestures at people.

"The truth?" I said. "In a word?" I brought my face close to his, but not too close. "Force!"

"What?"

"Force!" I repeated, "or rather, coercion!"

"What the devil are you talking about?"

"See Them over there?" I pointed a dramatic finger at the Bruise Brothers but kept it low, concealed behind my strawberry milk. "It was *Their* idea. All of it! They told me that if I didn't smear you, They'd kill me. I was acting in self-defense, Mr. Zimmerman. I was a puppet in Their hands. A puppet!"

The Music Man's eyes had expanded to doughnut dimensions, and I nodded gravely. I could almost make out the wheels of his mind grinding away in there.

He shook his head in disbelief. "George, this is more serious than I thought. For that kind of harassment, they would have been suspended, did you know that? Why didn't you come to me with this right away? I could have helped you. Now it's your word against theirs."

"So what do we do now?"

"I will talk to Mr. Harris about it, and then, of course, talk to your father when we arrive at school. But in the meantime," he bleated sternly, "I want you to use your very best manners in any dealings you may have with them. You're not exactly off the hook here. Not until we've gotten this thing settled, anyway."

He got up, and I did, too, to trail him the way a duckling trails the wide backside of its mother duck, first to unload my tray in the dirty-tray receptacle, then to follow him out the door. I shadowed him pretty closely, but before I passed through the doorway, I turned to try out my very best manners for the first time.

I returned the wave of the Bruise Brothers, who were watching my exit intently, only my manners were so good that I used all *five* fingers in my wave, while each of Them felt it reasonable to extend only *one*. Then I hustled to catch up with my new bodyguard, feeling not altogether too bad.

Because the truth might very well have set me free.

18

MY BODYGUARD AND I AMBLED OUT INTO THE bright sunshine, and after a few paces Mr. Zimmerman stopped, looked around him, and said, "We should bring the truck back here before we do any more work on the sets. Then we can just load them in as we finish them. What do you think, George?"

"That works for me!" I replied. If he had suggested skipping through a bed of hot coals on our way to visit the quicksand, I would have agreed, for as long as we stuck together, I knew I'd be safe.

We walked quietly through the Compound, Mr. Zimmerman probably resolving to get to the bottom of things a little better next time before meting out justice so quickly, while I mused on Hurricane Judith, that queen of storms, thinking that while the future might not look so hot for our important sand dune system, it was looking pretty radiant for me.

When we got to the parking lot, a stunning silver Chevy S-10 pickup stood alone and majestic under the noonday sun. Again I marveled at how this man could possess such a macho vehicle. But when I noticed that instead of standard pinstriping, the truck had been decorated with a long, winding scale of musical notes, I decided I'd been a little too hasty in my judgment. The leopard hadn't changed his spots entirely.

The journey back was fun. The truck jogged along over the trail, and we bounced along inside it. Had I been a taller person, I probably would have arrived at journey's end with a skull fracture or two. But I enjoyed it. Not that we ran over anybody or anything, but it made me feel somehow important seeing kid after kid make a diving leap to get out of the way only to look up and see *my* smiling face in the window.

But since the trip back is always a lot faster than the trip going, it was soon time once again to hike up the sleeves, spit on the hands, and simulate getting down to work. There were sets to build and backdrops to paint, and by gosh, I was going to prove to my music teacher once and for all that I had no mechanical ability whatsoever so that he'd take his time and think long and hard before he would ever ask for my help again.

I would dazzle him with my ineptitude.

I read a poem once on how the best laid plans of mice and men almost never pan out for them, written by a poet who must have spent considerable time with Mr. Zimmerman, for he would assign me only simple tasks, such as painting his submarine-tank a basic gray, that even I couldn't foul up, try as I might. I gave the submarine-tank two lavish coats and left it to dry, then painted other boards whatever colors Mr. Z had directed—some that would represent atmospheric conditions with Sky Blue paint, tempestuous seas on other boards with Pollution Green paint—and I let these bake away in the sun. It was mindless work, really. My brain relaxed, and I forgot all about the world around me, until I climbed onto the tailgate to help load the dried boards into the truck and saw that the world around me had edged in a little closer than I would have liked.

I could see the Compound, and there were dozens of kids nearby, but my corrective lenses held my focus on only two—*Sam Toselli with his bulky arm draped across the delicate shoulders of Allison Picone*. Mr. Zimmerman had wandered off after mumbling something like "Okay, that's it, George. You can get down now," which I didn't really hear, and I stood there leaning on the particleboards, watching the two share what appeared to be an intimate laugh—until everything went dark. In my emotional anguish I had relaxed my grip on the backdrops, and the heavy boards came crashing down, knocking me over the side of the truck.

I lay there, dead in the sand, looking up into black space until sunlight emerged in a kind of spinning spiral. I knew then that I couldn't be dead after all, because the gruesome face of Brooke Walters suddenly formed the eye of the spinning spiral, and after a long career in Sunday school, I knew that a face such as hers could never be found in Heaven. I tried blinking the apparition away, but it leaned right over me, so I brought myself painfully to a sitting position and Brooke started squealing.

"Allison wants you to stop looking at her. She thinks it's weird."

What? She saw me staring? She must have seen me fall!

"I wasn't looking at her," I lied, reddening.

"You stare at her every day of your life, George. Stop it! She thinks you're WEIRD!" Then she made a face even more horrible than her normal one and strutted away.

Weird? I thought. *How am I weird?* I looked down at the ink sketch of the snail's reproductive parts on my knee. My pants had ripped there, and the snail seemed to be mocking me now. *Oh my God!* I realized. *I am weird!* I groaned and flopped back down on the sand, then groaned a second time when the big clumsy feet of my music teacher tripped over my legs. He went crashing to all fours, like a cartwheeling hippopotamus, sending a volley of sand into my face.

"George!" he cried after he'd stopped wheezing. "What happened? Did you fall down?"

I might have asked him that, but I didn't, because there was sand up my nose. So I just offered him a gurgle.

Now, you're not supposed to yank an accident victim by the arm and haul him to his feet and then start whacking him with your flabby palms to get the sand off him, but Mr. Zimmerman must have missed the class on basic first aid because that's exactly what he did.

"Did you lose your balance up there?"

I nodded slowly.

"Well, nothing seems to be broken. Do you want me to take you to the nurse?"

I shook my head vigorously. I did not want to go out into the Compound and have people look at me, one person in particular. For Mr. Zimmerman had been wrong, part of me *had* broken, and Nurse Kobb would never have been able to fix my broken heart, not even with a dozen Ace bandages.

"Then why don't you just rest awhile," he said. Together we limped over to the wall, and I sat down under the shady overhang of the mess hall roof. Mr. Z stood gazing at me with such tender concern in his eyes that I almost laughed out loud. Then I remembered that my life's dream considered me weird and let out another groan instead.

"Is there something I can get for you, George?" he asked.

"How about a little ginger ale," I replied, really more for his benefit than mine. He looked like he was going to start wringing his hands if I didn't give him something useful to do.

After he shoved off, I unzipped my backpack and very nearly put my headphones to my ears until I remembered that music would only remind me of Allison. Not that the two of us ever had a "song," per se, but she'd been on my mind so much since the second grade that basically every song I'd ever listened to, I'd listened to while thinking of her. So in a sense you could say we had thousands of songs.

I reached for *A Tale of Two Cities* instead, and such were my amazing powers of concentration that when I got to the page I had marked, I was absorbed within seconds in the classic Charles-being-drugged-in-his-prison-cell scene. So absorbed that when my drink order arrived, I think I waved it aside with a careless hand and mumbled something about leaving the man a handsome tip.

I was at my favorite part in the whole book. The part where the imposter prisoner, Sydney Carton, meets up with a fellow prisoner, a poor little seamstress with a sweet, spare face. And instead of telling the man, "I think you're weird," the lovely creature asks only to hold his brave hand. When they step out of the tumbrel, Sydney Carton says to her, "Keep your eyes open upon me, dear child," and, in a spirit of gallantry, lets her go *first* to the guillotine. I knew right then that in spite of my aching heart, I would have done no less for Allison Picone—such was my undying devotion.

My conscious mind was immersed in the book, but my subconscious mind noticed out of the corner of its eye that the Music Man was still close at hand. I was maybe ten feet away from the end of the building, and he was standing at the corner talking to a person or persons unknown, hidden by the adjoining wall. It struck me as odd because no one *ever* talked to him. Not even the other teachers. The guy was a lone wolf.

They must have been discussing my accident because his eloquent hand gestures seemed to illustrate the *George Falling Out of the Truck* story. I heard the Bruder's motherly voice say, "Poor little George. That's too bad," and saw Mr. Zimmerman limp off over the horizon. As I continued to read, the thought crossed my mind that I would probably be receiving a get-well plant from that kind lady before very long, but what I heard next made the words on the printed page dance and blur between my hands.

"Well! That was fun to watch. It's a shame he didn't break his neck, though. I would have paid to see that."

It was Mrs. Love's voice. There was no mistaking it.

Then Mrs. Bruder's kind, motherly voice said, "Look on the bright side, Marjorie. It knocked the wind out of him. It may have knocked some of the conceit out of him, too!"

I froze against the wall and stopped breathing. They were talking about me.

Then I heard Mr. Caruso.

"I'd sure like to knock the wind out of that know-it-all myself! Except Mr. Clark would have my head on a platter. So I just smile and nod . . . even though I'd like to strangle him."

"He's pretentious!" a heated male voice chimed in, but I couldn't identify it because my ears felt suddenly on fire. "He's obnoxious! Completely obnoxious! The 'authority' on everything. Altogether too pleased with himself! Thank God this is his last year."

"It's going to be a very long year."

"Oh, he's not *that* bad," said the Bruder, defending me. I thought, *Not that bad? Whatever happened to gumdrop with a capital "G"?*

"He is *that* bad! He's pompous and overbearing!"

"Still, he *is* gifted," said Mrs. Love thoughtfully, summing me up in her own neat way. "I suppose Mr. Clark thinks we're lucky to have him."

Her words seemed to hang in the air as the teachers mulled this over, or maybe they'd only paused in order to curse me under their collective breath. I didn't really know.

What I did know was that time stood still, and for a long while I just sat there. Not thinking. I couldn't think. It was like I was numb all over. If somebody had come along and kicked me hard in the stomach, I probably wouldn't have felt it.

So I just sat there.

19

THERE'S NO TELLING HOW LONG I MIGHT HAVE sat there. What brought me morosely to my feet were the words, "Gifted? He's just a pompous snot with a superiority complex!" uttered passionately by that anonymous male voice. I got up slowly and, taking the long way around the mess hall, staggered off in a daze to the solitude of Cabin F. I'd left my ginger ale untouched in the sand. It must have been its discovery that made my music teacher come looking for me.

I don't know how he found me. I had become as invisible as possible, buried deep inside my sleeping bag with just the tip of my nose sticking out. I would have kept that inside, too, and zipped the bag up over my head and let that be the end of that except I didn't think I'd have the stamina. I'd just have to let Sam and Jason finish me off in Their own way whenever They had the time. Granted, Their way would not be quite as neat as my way would have been, but I felt sure it would be considerably quicker. I would leave it to the experts and make everybody happy. Suddenly a hand shook my shoulder.

"George, you need to see the nurse. No arguments now. I can see that you're hurt."

"I'm not hurt."

"Then what's the problem?"

The problem? My mind had just flashed *The George R. Clark Story: Random Scenes from the Past.* Stupid memories like Mr. Caruso sitting beside me on the bench and agreeing that any idiot could hit a line drive but it took a special person to keep the score as neatly and as accurately as I did. *The big liar.* But one could expect as much from a man who chewed the same wad of gum twenty-four seven, even while sucking down Gatorade. A man whose cross-trainers were always sparkling white because he never took part in his own war games. He was just a clapper and a whistler! A pair of ladies' four-inch stiletto heels would have served him just as well! I didn't care what he thought.

What *hurt* was remembering all the time I'd spent in the science lab with Mrs. Love. And all the talks. Deep, intellectual talks, usually about something I'd just read in *Popular Science* involving two-headed livestock. Come to think of it, Mrs. Love had never really said much when we'd talked, but she'd always looked awfully enthralled. At least she'd moved her eyebrows up and down a lot as I spoke. Now I knew she was just praying silently that when the bell rang, I would go home and trip over a rug wrinkle and break my neck. She would have paid to see that. *Oh my God!*

And all the carefully misspelled notes slid through the vents in my locker asking me to make the world a better place and just die already. I had always imagined they were from some of the more academically impaired members of the student body. Now I wasn't so sure. They might easily have been put there by the begemmed hand of Mrs. Bruder after a couple of swift looks over her shoulder.

I could have kicked myself for being so gullible. And I would have done so had my sleeping bag provided more leg room. It was humiliating! The whole world had lined up against me, and now I had nobody. Even Anita was gone. Well, I would never go back to that school again. Not ever. I'd find a new school where people would appreciate me, and I'd kiss these jerks good-bye. Metaphorically speaking, of course.

The Music Man was patting my back, so I dried my face and rolled over to look at him. His eyes held none of the hostility I'd grown so accustomed to, only kindness now, and his gleaming cranium seemed to shimmer with newfound compassion. Even his coffee-stain mustache seemed concerned. He leaned forward.

"Tell me what's wrong, George."

I sighed. Here stood the one teacher who had never troubled to hide his feelings of disgust for me, and I had been ungrateful. Those had been good times. I should have treasured him, for he was an *honest* man. Pitiful, but honest, and I would miss him in a way.

"Mr. Zimmerman," I announced, sitting up. "I've given the matter a lot of thought, and I've decided I won't be going back to school."

He looked surprised. "You like it here that much?"

"No. What I mean is Conrad T. Parks has seen the last of George R. Clark. I'm going to transfer to a private school."

"When did you decide this?"

"Just now. You see, Parks Middle School fails to address my needs properly. I know my parents are trying to mainstream me, but it isn't working. I need to be with my own kind. Nobody's fault, really." I gave his arm a return pat. "These things happen."

"If you're worried about Jason Barton and Sam Toselli . . ."

"Oh, They don't enter into it at all."

"I want you to know that I've had a talk with those two. They denied your story about what happened last night. Denied it categorically. They said putting mustard on me was entirely your idea, that they knew nothing about it."

"Is that a fact," I said bitterly.

"But I didn't believe them. I didn't believe them, because I believe you, George."

I gazed at him with new eyes. How I could have described his face as "revolting" was beyond me. It was really just mildly unappealing.

"And," he went on, "I've had a talk with Mr. Harris. Sam Toselli and his gang will no longer be staying in Cabin F. We thought it better to separate them from you tonight, and Mr. Caruso very cordially accepted them into his cabin. Five of his boys will be moving here into ours."

Well, I guess that was something, but it didn't make me feel as good as it should have. I sighed and let my head fall to my pillow with a bang. I'd left my CD player underneath it.

"So, do you still want to leave us, George?"

"It isn't about that," I said, sitting up, rubbing my head. "Really. I'm just mentally unstimulated. And I'm beginning to get headaches. Which is why I think I fell down out there." I couldn't tell him what I'd heard. It was too embarrassing.

"You fell down because you're mentally unstimulated?"

"Yes, and it catches me right here." I massaged my temples. "It's very painful."

"George, there's something you're not telling me."

"Fine," I snapped, dropping the pretense. "Would you believe it's because everyone here hates my guts? It takes a lot out of a person, being hated and everything."

Mr. Z nodded. "You get used to it. But that's not entirely true, is it? You still have your girlfriend, Anita Newell. She doesn't hate you. It seems rather the opposite to me."

Honestly! And for the last time! "She is NOT my girlfriend! And we're not friends anymore."

"But you two seemed so close," he persisted.

"Not anymore."

"Did you have a fight?"

"No."

"Then what happened?"

"I don't care to discuss it."

"Well, then," Mr. Z said, "we won't."

There followed a brief moment of silence, a nice peaceful moment that was interrupted by the sound a bunk bed makes when it is straining under a fleshy music teacher who's just taken a flying leap to the top. I clutched the rocking sidebars as Mr. Z maneuvered himself until he was sitting beside me with his legs dangling over the side. It appeared that we were going to have a cozy chat. The Music Man must have thought that he'd finally found a friend . . . in me, of all people! I dropped my head to my pillow with a quiet moan.

"Anita Newell," he murmured, obviously thinking I was upset over her. "You know what's funny, George?"

"I thought we weren't going to discuss it."

"Oh, we're not, we're not. I was just going to say that Anita Newell reminds me very much of a girl I used to know. A girl who was *my* best childhood friend. Same hair, same figure, same . . . oh . . . awkwardness."

"Are you going somewhere with this?"

"I was just remembering how surprised I was by her transformation. How surprised *she* was. It happened in high school."

"*What* happened in high school?"

"Why, her metamorphosis! One day that chrysalis—her awkward, ungainly, schoolgirl chrysalis—just sort of fell away, and out of it emerged a butterfly. A strikingly beautiful butterfly, I might add. A thing worth waiting for." He eyed me meaningfully. Then his mustache twitched at me meaningfully.

This was too much.

"As far as I'm concerned, Anita can stay in her cocoon until she rots! We aren't friends anymore. She happens to be disloyal," I told him by way of explanation. "And if she has to live out the rest of her days as a caterpillar, I couldn't care less!"

"I'm sorry to hear that," he said. Then he smiled. "You know what else is funny, George? I've never noticed it before, but you remind me very much of myself when I was your age."

"Funny," he says!

"And I'm glad I had the opportunity to punish you today because it's given me the chance to get to know you. I hope you don't leave us now. If you're worried about Sam and Jason, believe me when I tell you that I've faced my share of bullies in my younger days, and the only thing to do is to stand up to them." He raised his fist. "Stand tall! Face your fears and overcome them. Never let a group of bullies decide your fate. Do you know what Beethoven said? He said, 'I want to seize fate by the throat,' and that's just what you should do. Seize it by the throat!"

"Is that what you did when you came to work at our school? Seized fate by the throat?" I asked him. The Music Man looked so taken aback that I immediately wished I could have taken it back. I tried to soften the sting.

"I mean, we're really glad you did, of course."

"Well . . ." he said, staring off into space for some time, "it wasn't quite what I'd envisioned for myself. But . . ." After another long moment he shook his head and looked down at his watch. "It's five thirty, George, and I am keeping you from your dinner. The time has come for you to join your classmates in the dining hall." He lowered himself to the floor. "You are officially off the hook."

He was leaving me!

"Mr. Zimmerman! Wait! I'm not hungry. We could finish the sets together. I like working with you. I'd like to work with you all night!"

"That's very kind of you, George, but my esteemed colleagues feel my talents can best be utilized elsewhere. I am required to pack up our food stores and cooking supplies for our evacuation in the morning. So for now, you and I must part company.

"But if you want my advice," he said from the doorway, "you'll stand up to those bullies and show them they have no power over you. And you'll make up with Anita. Because in this world, George, if you're lucky enough to find a friend, you must be very careful not to lose her. A good friend is the greatest gift you'll ever have."

WITH THE MUSIC MAN GONE, I LAY BACK down on my bunk in a sullen mood, so sullen that when a big black water bug crawled across the ceiling to a spot over my bed, I never thought to fly off the bunk in terror as I would have done under everyday circumstances. Instead, I slid down into my sleeping bag and gave myself up to some pretty deep thinking. But all I could think deeply about was food. Because I'd lied about not being hungry, and the tantalizing aroma of chicken patty on a roll with zesty potato rounds and mouthwatering carrot coins wafting at me through the open doorway was too much to bear. I reached inside my jacket and counted them: thirteen Hershey bars left, but two would suffice. I rolled onto my stomach and ate one, and was just unwrapping the second when it occurred to me that a little dinner music might be nice.

I slid my hand under my pillow to pull out my CD player, but what I pulled out looked very little like a CD player and much more like a rock. A rock with a note taped to it. A note that read, "YOUR TIME WILL COME, WORM!"

I gasped. The Bruise Brothers were on the prowl.

Well, I would take Mr. Z's advice. I would apologize to Anita. Because Anita, being a girl, could stay mad indefinitely unless you said you were sorry, but then she'd melt like butter, and I would stick with her until lights-out. Now, finding Anita and apologizing would carry its own risks, a woman scorned, et cetera, but it was a chance I would have to take.

Bathed in twilight's glow, the Compound was eerily silent as I crept out of the cabin and raced furtively to a clump of bayberry bushes growing conveniently between Cabin F and the mess hall. I knelt behind the shrubbery in order to catch my breath. Not a soul to be seen. *So far so good.* I counted to three and with a burst of speed made it all the way to the building. With my body flat against the wall, I leaned into the open window, the very window Sam and Jason had terrorized me through at lunchtime, just far enough to let half an eyeball inspect the room.

One hundred seventy-nine student bodies were massed inside. Anita was sitting alone at the table Mr. Z and I had occupied earlier, doubtless in memory of me. Anita always had a sentimental streak. I tried whistling to get her attention, but my whistle got lost in the din, so I reached inside my jacket, felt around for a chocolate bar, then deftly lobbed one in her direction. The missile sailed through the air in a soft and graceful arc before it crash-landed onto Anita's dinner tray, causing an upsurge of tomato soup to mantle her face. She vaulted off the bench with an agility I found impressive for a girl her size and stood glaring at me through the window, her eyes flashing fire. I gave her a little wave and watched her disappear from view.

Then through the doorway she came, marching straight into the Compound, looking neither left nor right. I hustled to catch up with her and, when I reached her side, tried to break the ice with "And there's plenty more where *that* came from!" in reference to her fondness for chocolate, but she wasn't having any. Without turning her head, she plowed straight into her cabin, plowed back out carrying a girlish-looking traveling case and a towel, then plowed into the girls' latrine, still ignoring me even though I matched her pace, stride for stride.

I waited for her to come out, but she was taking forever. Since there was no one around, I decided in desperation to be daring once again. I edged in backward through the door and, knowing the layout as I did, made my way without misadventure to the main room. Anita was there wearing the bath towel wrapped around her head, leaning over a sink with her face close to the mirror.

"Hi!" I said brightly.

Anita jumped two feet off the floor. "George!" she cried, spinning around. "What do you think you're doing!"

Then I jumped even higher than she had.

"What do you think *you're* doing?" Her face was covered in a thick white paste. She might have warned me.

"This is the *girls' room!* You're going to get us both in trouble!" She came toward me and, using both hands, slammed me into one of the stalls and swung the door shut behind us. She stood with her hands on her hips, her eyes were glittering, and I could tell right away that forgiveness would not come in a snap.

"I am really, really sorry," I said. "I really, really am."

Anita said nothing. She just kept looking at me as though she were waiting for me to say the magic word or something.

"*Please* don't be mad anymore. I need your friendship right now. My life is in danger out there."

"Your life is in danger in here, George," she said in a really menacing way, and I'll admit frankly that I shivered. Anita's face, seen in its natural state, is a little scary, but her face covered in all that goop was straight out of the pages of Stephen King. "You are the biggest jerk that ever lived. All you ever think about is yourself, and *that's* why everyone hates you!"

I took her comments silently because I was still shivering, which must have moved Anita to pity for her eyes softened a bit. "I don't mean to hurt your feelings, though."

"Thank you," I said, "that's very big of you." We stood quietly for a moment.

"Just answer me this. Is everything about you, George? Everything?"

I cupped my chin. I had to think about that. I guess I thought about it too long because she suddenly got surly again.

"Just go! Get out of here before we get caught!" Then she more or less catapulted me through the swing door, and I would have kept right on going except I heard a shriek of feminine laughter that stopped me in my tracks. The girls' latrine, which had probably stood empty for hours, had suddenly become Studio 54. I made a diving leap back into the stall. There had to have been a dozen girls out there, judging by the number of feet sashaying under the door, and I wasn't going anywhere.

I will say this for Anita. When push comes to shove,

she can display the qualities of a true friend even while hating my guts. She could so easily have pushed me or shoved me right back out there to meet my doom, exposing me, so to speak, to the female populace, but she didn't. Instead, she grabbed me roughly around my midsection and hoisted me feet first onto the commode, commanding me with a whispered, "Bend down and don't fall in," which I was happy to obey. I set my backpack on the lid of the tank before it could throw off my center of gravity and made like a statue.

Anita stood at the door with her eye to the crack. I couldn't tell what was going on out there, but the noise made me think of a tickle fight in a henhouse. Lots of earsplitting revelry. Through the giggles and the whispers I thought I could detect some serious nail polish discussions, but my powers of observation were pretty limited. We stayed that way for God knows how long, and the crick developing in my lumbar region was becoming fairly pronounced when I heard the latrine door open abruptly, as if an express train had hit it.

"GIRLS!"

A hush fell over the room. Anita turned to me with wide eyes.

"You have THREE seconds! Just THREE seconds before you ladies receive ZEROS for the Scavenger Hunt! Starting now!" Strong words from Miss Dixon, our robust health teacher, who must have stood there in her legendary pose, tapping her legendary foot. All we heard then were the sounds of scurrying feet and the heavy latrine door banging at intervals.

Finally, all was quiet. "Let's give it a minute," Anita whispered, "before we go."

I nodded, relaxing my posture. I sat down on top of

the tank to wait, and learned that the minute was up when Anita wrenched me down from the plumbing and snarled, "Now get lost."

"Wait!" I begged. "I need to talk to you!"

"We'll talk at the Scavenger Hunt. You might not be getting a grade for this, George, but I am."

"But I can't go to the Scavenger Hunt. They're going to kill me out there! I mean it! I need your help!"

"Okay, okay," she said. "I'll meet you then. You go first and wait for me at the watchtower. I'll get there as soon as I can. But then *I* have to participate, George, even if *you* don't. And you're making me late. So get moving!"

I nodded happily and, with my best friend's assistance, shot out of the stall like a leaping jackrabbit and hared it all the way to the observation tower.

Not knowing, of course, that a pair of callous ears in the adjacent stall had taken careful note of our plan and that my enemies would soon be making plans of Their own.

21

HARING IT TO THE OBSERVATION TOWER TOOK me along a brief stretch of shoreline—a rather dirty brief stretch of shoreline littered with seaweed, driftwood, and countless jellyfish, which from a distance looked like innocent soggy plastic bags but up close scared the bejesus out of me.

Still, it was heartening to see signs of Hurricane Judith and to know that in fourteen hours we would be hitting the road. Because all this fleeing from danger was exhausting. I just wanted to go home. I missed my mom like crazy. I pictured her face, her sympathetic smile, her kind worry lines. It brought a lump to my throat. I imagined us in our cozy kitchen over steaming mugs of cocoa, catching up on lost time and looking into private schools—because that's what I needed—a fresh start. With a fresh start I would do everything differently. I'd be cool from day one, which would require a whole new wardrobe and possibly different hair. And I'd be popular. In the classroom I would go for the cheap laughs instead of the more erudite jokes that only I understood. The words "yo" and "later" would replace my "hello" and "good-bye," and every individual I addressed would be known to me only as "dude," regardless of age, sex, or social standing. And that was just the beginning. With a bit more planning, there was no telling how far my coolness would go.

I was just considering the wisdom of getting a tattoo, maybe something along the lines of the periodic table of elements, when my thoughts returned sharply to the dismal present. The tower loomed in the foreground—seventy-five feet of steel-reinforced cement rising gray and formidable against the darkening sky. I wondered if it might be safer to go inside, climb the one hundred and fourteen steps to the top, and wait for Anita there, but thought better of it. According to the film we saw, the tower walls were a foot thick and had two rows of viewing ports positioned at thirty-nine-degree intervals. A fine defense if you were facing the Nazis, but would it protect me from the Bruise Brothers? They might easily ambush me up there. I would take my chances on the ground.

I sat down facing the bay, with my back to the tower, trying to relax, but it was pointless. My body was set on high alert. My pulse raced, every noise made me jump, and when a local bird of indeterminate species exploded out of the trees behind me, my heart crashed into my rib cage and hammered on it for the next five minutes. You could say I was feeling a bit tense. Which is why when I heard the distinct sound of a person going, *"Pssst,"* behind me, I almost bit my tongue in half. I turned my head. It was coming from the woods.

"Pssst! Hey George. Over here."

A feminine voice. Was it Anita's? *No,* I decided, *it's much too feminine.* I sat up straight and squinted into the trees. It was getting dark, and the forest was comparatively black.

"George!"

I squinted harder and sat up straighter, then felt a thrill of elation as a halo of light moved to the edge of the beach. "I need you," a musical voice called softly. "I'm all by myself, and I'm not good at finding things."

It was Allison Picone, her yellow hair twinkling like fairy gold in the twilight. She was beckoning me with a dainty flashlight clasped in a dainty hand. Her other hand held a paper grocery bag and an itemized list.

"Will you help me, George?" she begged.

Now I should have been suspicious. I should have asked myself right away, *Where are the Ugly Girlfriends?* But instead I thought, *So, I'm weird, am I? Brooke Walters made the whole thing up. Guess we'll see who's weird now!* And I leaped to my feet and skipped merrily into the trees. Inside the forest, though, I lost sight of Allison.

"Where are you?" I called into the gloom.

I glimpsed her waving to me from some distance away, but when I got there, I found she'd vanished again. *Aha! Playing hard to get,* I decided, for I knew that women were apt to do that in the heat of the chase. At least they were in books, anyway. Throwing caution to the wind, I followed the elusive beam of light in and out of the trees, letting it lead me deeper and deeper into the forest.

A little *too* deep.

"Stand still a minute," I called, stumbling, "or at least slow down." I couldn't help feeling irritated. It was like playing cat and mouse, only the mouse had her own flashlight and the cat kept getting tangled up in pricker bushes.

I was just disentangling myself from an especially nasty one when I heard a sound. The sound of rampaging wildebeests crashing through the forest. I froze in mid-bush. *It was the Bruise Brothers.*

"He's right over there!" a bell-like voice rang out, followed by a peal of heartless laughter that I had once considered musical. I was devastated. Too devastated to think clearly. So I let panic take over and did what came naturally. I hunkered down into the bush and prayed, silently and hard.

22

"WHERE'S HE AT?"

"Did you see him?"

"He's gotta be around here somewhere."

From my hiding place, I watched Them, five apelike silhouettes in conference just a few yards away. I didn't move a muscle. My breathing I kept to the barest minimum.

"Maybe he ran off."

"No, we woulda seen him. He's here someplace."

A bit of shrewd deductive reasoning coming from Gabriel Arno, whose bulky form was so close to me I could have reached out and touched it. Not that I would have. Then the snap of a twig in the near vicinity caused Them to fall silent and me to gulp. I stared hard in the direction the noise had come from. It was Anita, lumbering alone under the trees, wearing *her* black aviator jacket and carrying my backpack, which I had left in the girls' latrine. I feared for her safety, with her hair pinned back in a bun and wearing my same getup. Now, any human being with a brain could see that it wasn't me, but would *They* know the difference?

In the next instant my fears were realized. Gabriel Arno's thirst for my blood must have clouded his vision. There was a rush of feet and a flurry of fists. He'd jumped her. Anita fell to the ground like a stricken fawn.

The Bruise Brothers were on him like a pack of wolves, trying to pull him off. "That's not him, you idiot! Get up! That's Anita New-Face!"

It took a moment for this to penetrate Gabriel's thick skull. Then he sprang up with a startled oath and took off like a shot, joining his teammates in Their flight through the woods. Anita just lay like a crumpled leaf. I crawled out of the bush and made my way over to her.

"What on earth happened to you?" I cried.

Anita blinked at me. "Where were you?"

"Far away, but I sensed danger. Can you stand up?"

"I don't know," she whispered hoarsely.

I wrapped my arms around her and pulled her to her feet. "He must have hit you pretty hard."

"I thought you were *far away*." She eyed me narrowly. "You were right over there, weren't you? I thought I saw your beady little eyes."

"You did not see my beady little eyes. You couldn't have seen them because they were waiting over at the tower for *you*." I steadied my voice, which tends to shake when I lie. "It might have been a squirrel you saw or a sea turtle, but it was definitely *not* me."

"You weren't at the tower, George. I went there first. Then I got worried and came looking for you."

That made me gulp. But I looked her squarely in the eye and said resolutely, "I was inside, at the top. Honest! And then *I* got worried and came looking for you."

"Forget it," she sighed. "Take me to the nurse. I think my nose is bleeding."

We plodded onward through the trees and I snuck a glance at Anita. Blood trickled from her nose. Her cheeks were puffy, and her hair was a tangled mess of brown frizz and pine needles. I thought, *Of all the luck! Poor Anita!* The fact that her bad luck had been my good luck I refused to think about.

The plan was for me to escort Anita to the nurse, then sit outside the door to wait for her in the darkness until she came out. But as I was fulfilling my part of the second part it hit me that the darkness had suddenly become *really* dark and until the Bruise Brothers were taken into custody, it would do Anita no good to have me get beaten up as well.

So I made my way over to the safe confines of Cabin F, where I saw that my bunkmates were packing their bags. I joined them, feeling relieved for the first time all day. We would soon be going home.

And later, when I'd learned from Mr. Z that the Bruise Brothers would certainly be expelled for what They'd done to Anita, I snuggled down into my sleeping bag and let sleep wash over me in a soothing wave, calm and peaceful at last.

Not realizing, of course, that what I was feeling was the calm before the storm.

23

I SLEPT LIKE A BABY ALL THROUGH THE NIGHT, then fitfully as dawn approached, like a baby having a nightmare. For a nightmare was what I had.

It started out as a good dream, one I remembered having had before. I was in my bedroom, except my bedroom had turned into an enormous laboratory—a real state-of-the-art laboratory with the latest high-tech equipment and plenty of menials bustling around doing the grunt work. And there I was, in the very center of things, standing at a podium and describing my latest research on mitochondrial DNA, with my lovely assistant by my side. My lovely assistant was usually Allison Picone in these dreams, but in this one it was Mr. Zimmerman, which should have tipped me off right away that things were going to get ugly.

But as I said, at first it was a good dream. I was much older, tall and distinguished, impeccable in my white lab coat and looking a heck of a lot like Brad Pitt. The press was there, gathered around and straining to pick up my every word; even the president was there. And I had made a colossal discovery. I had come upon a particular strand of DNA that indicated a strong evolutionary relationship between the common chimp, the pygmy chimp, a certain rare subspecies of orangutan, and a number of key offensive linemen in the NFL. The genetic consistency was startling, and the ramifications would shake the scientific community, not to mention Monday Night Football, to its very foundations. Journalists' pens were scratching feverishly at tablets and flashbulbs were flashing away when suddenly Sam Toselli elbowed his way through the crowd and got right in my face.

"Why didn't you tell me my Junior Scientist project was no good? You watched me work on it for months, pretending to help me, knowing the whole time that it wouldn't work. I embarrassed myself in front of everybody, and you let me!" He balled up his fists, ready to strike. "I thought we were friends."

"Sam!" I cried. "We are friends!"

I stepped back and raised my hand in a peace gesture, feeling sure he wouldn't hit a man wearing sunglasses, but he stepped forward as I stepped back. Behind me I felt Mr. Zimmerman blocking my retreat. "You have to face your fears, George," he muttered in my ear, "if you want to overcome them!"

"You wanted to make me look stupid," Sam bellowed, "just to make yourself look smart! I trusted you! I wanted to be like you!"

I shrank back, just avoiding his blow, and, turning around, felt a surprising burst of courage—because the Music Man had turned into Anita. I got behind her and tried to remember what his project had been about. Had it something to do with animal behavior? Was it "How High Can a Dog Count?"

"It was hardly my fault," I told him bravely, over Anita's shoulder. "Your findings were inconclusive, your presentation ill-prepared, and your methods lacked vision. I believe the dog may have, too." But even as I said this, my conscious mind knew it wasn't right. His project had been called "How Airplanes Fly: A Demonstration of Bernoulli's Principle" and used paper airplanes. And it would have been impressive, too, had his airplanes not had kamikaze tendencies.

Sam lunged forward, grabbed me by the throat, and began shaking me hard, dislodging my teeth and sending them rattling around in my mouth. Harder and harder he shook, and the rattling got louder and louder until I woke up panting. I could still hear the rattling noise. It was the wind blowing hard against the cabin windows, and as I lay on my bunk fully awake, the gusts sounded like waves crashing on the beach right outside our door.

Hurricane Judith had come early.

24

I JUMPED OUT OF BED TO CHECK OUT THE weather, forgetting for the moment that I was on the second story, and it must have been my subsequent fall to the floor that woke my sleeping bunkmates. But wake they did. As I hobbled painfully over to the nearest window, one by one they got up to join me, having caught my excitement like a contagious illness.

You know, there's nothing like severe weather to bring people together and give them a shared sense of respect for the mighty forces of nature. The ten boys of Cabin F stood united in the window, awed and spellbound, watching the wind blow a heavy yellow garbage can onto its side, then roll it across the Compound with enough velocity to knock an unsuspecting Mrs. Love, who was outside the female latrine, off her feet. The ground was still dry at this point, or it would have been even better.

The rain began to fall as Mr. Zimmerman served our breakfast, a nutritious bran muffin and a warm box of apple juice, which we consumed just as the electricity went out. While we ate, the Music Man paced the room, already draped in a navy blue rain poncho that billowed like the plumage of a bird, the guy ready to bug out at a moment's notice.

Our bags were packed, piled in a heap on the floor, and we were told to sit as far away from the two windows as we could. So, naturally, all ten of us crowded on Mr. Z's cot. We had our flashlights out and spent half the time making shadow puppets on the wall and the other half training the beams to fall on Mr. Z's expansive scalp area. When two or three of my bunkmates sniffed the air dramatically, claiming that they could still smell the mustard, the Music Man broke the party mood with a shake of his luminous dome.

"Knock it off!" He raised a navy blue wing in warning. "Just eat your food. We'll be leaving any minute." He glanced fearfully at the window, at the glass dancing in the frame. He checked his watch for possibly the hundredth time, and when that ceased to satisfy, he started pacing again. Sensing his anxiety and being in a mellow mood myself, I invited him to come over and join us—take a load off, as it were—not intending my usual offense.

"Thank you, no," he bleated irritably. "I prefer to stand."

"It's just a storm, Mr. Zimmerman," I said. "Don't worry. I've seen bigger."

"Just a storm? Have you ever witnessed a hurricane before? Obviously not," he snapped, answering his own question, "or you wouldn't call it 'just a storm,' let me tell you."

"Have you ever witnessed a hurricane, Mr. Zimmerman?" a voice asked behind me.

"As a matter of fact, yes, I have. Hurricane Donna,

which happened to strike New England on September 12, 1960, to become the fifth strongest hurricane of record to hit the United States. My family was summering in Rhode Island," he explained, "a part of this country where we believed a hurricane making landfall to be as likely an event as a blizzard hitting Miami in July. Consequently, we did not take the warnings seriously. We thought it would be 'just a storm,' too, and by the time we tried to evacuate, we couldn't. All the roads had closed. We nearly died in that hurricane," he continued, softly. "I was five years old. It was the most horrifying experience I ever hope to have."

Everyone got quiet. I did, too, in order to do the math, and as the Music Man droned on, it occurred to me that he was fifty years old—much older than I ever would have thought. I stared at him. He'd always seemed sort of young and peevish to me. Maybe not in his first youth, more like his second or third. It just goes to show how little you know about a person.

"The floors were shaking." He demonstrated with his hands. "The walls were wobbling. The pressure got so low that it sucked the water from the toilet just like a vacuum, and we huddled there in the bathroom for five hours in the dark, listening to glass breaking all over the house; pictures falling from the walls; furniture crashing together; our roof, the neighbors' roofs, ripping off. . . ." He shook his head, remembering. "It was terrifying. Absolutely terrifying. Something I do not intend to experience twice."

He studied the window again, with understandable fear in his eyes. None of us knew what to say. We sat quietly, following his gaze, nobody moving, until a tree branch smacked the glass and we all jumped.

The Music Man checked his watch.

"Eight thirty. Traffic. It must be traffic," he said more to himself than to us. "The buses are coming, but they must be stuck in traffic."

He started pacing again.

At precisely nine thirty we were told by a rather moist Mr. Harris that the buses had arrived, and by that time the rain was falling in sheets.

We put on our rain gear, those of us who'd remembered to pack any, that is. I found a bright yellow rain slicker in my bag with an insulated foul-weather hood, and when I say "bright," what I mean is radioactive. I shoved it back in before anyone else saw it. I think I would have drawn fewer horrified stares prancing all the way to the parking lot in the nude. I put on my black aviator jacket instead and made a mental note that if I ever went off to camp again, I would definitely pack for myself. Not that I would ever go off to camp again. Still, I couldn't wait to test my new waterproof field-and-stream boots, featuring slip-on convenience and an optional toe warmer, the temperature of one's toes being critical at times like these.

We grabbed our bags. I tried to balance my duffel bag and sleeping roll symmetrically, one on each hip like a good pack mule, when I noticed my backpack was missing. I had never taken it back from Anita following her *melee* in the woods.

I looked for her as the eighth grade made a mad dash to the parking lot. The buses were there in a long line opposite Mr. Zimmerman's pickup truck, the bed now dressed in a flapping blue tarp to protect our backdrops. With my jacket over my head, its fuzzy collar serving as a sort of visor and keeping my glasses fairly dry, I surveyed the scene.

It was utter chaos. Students were pushing each other up the steps, really fighting to get on first, while teachers, hanging on to the bus doors for dear life, pretended to find their students' names and check them off lists. I spotted Anita making for the last bus in line and ran to catch up with her.

"Hello!" I screamed into her ear, hoping to be heard over the wind. Anita gave a hop as if electrocuted, and when her feet touched down, she slowly turned around, and my eyes nearly popped their sockets. She looked *ghastly*. Her left eye was purple with bruises, and there was a big yellow bump on the lid. It hurt me just to look at it.

"Boy, am I glad I found you!" I shouted. "I was getting really worried!" I dropped my bags and put an arm around her neck, placing a tender hand on her shoulder in case I should reel. A look of pure gratitude flowed from her eyes. At least it flowed from the right eye. I wasn't about to look at the left one again.

"I've been looking all over for you!" I yelled. "I hope you still have my backpack! I've missed it like crazy!"

The right eye stared at me for a long time and her mouth opened, but no words came out. I wondered if the beating had given her a concussion. She looked brain-affected. I was about to repeat myself, only slower and clearer so that the words might penetrate, when she suddenly sprang to life.

"Your backpack?"

I nodded.

"You were worried about your backpack?"

I nodded again. She was slow, but she was getting the picture.

"Ask Mr. Harris!" she shrieked, causing me to bound backward and the people around us to stare. "He took it from me last night, after you ran off and left me! You want to know something, George?" she said evenly, but with an evil glint in her good eye. "I wish they had gotten you. You are the meanest person I've ever met. You don't care about anyone but yourself. I hope one day you wake up and find out what you're really like! Because then you'll have nobody! And it'll be too late!" She spun on her heel and stomped up the steps of the bus.

I shook my head. Anita was having another mood, which meant I would be getting the silent treatment again. For two hours and fifty-seven minutes. My book and my CD player would make all the difference, especially since the thought of gazing at the back of Allison Picone's head no longer appealed to me. I would have to retrieve my backpack.

I stepped back to have a look around. I fought the wind and took a little jog down the line of buses, but there wasn't a single bow tie in the vicinity. Mr. Harris hadn't come up from the campground yet. I did, however, catch a glimpse of Drew Lewis and Tim Simpson looking like a couple of drowned rats on Their way to the stockade. I stopped to see which bus They got on. The other felons were no doubt already on it, and in a morbid way I thought it would have been kind of nice to take a last look at Them—a last smug look.

I was to change my mind a moment later.

25

WITH CAMPERS STILL POURING INTO THE parking lot, I decided I'd scoot over to the pathway so as to be right on the spot whenever Mr. Harris emerged, my impulsive nature once again leading me astray and trying to get me killed. The path had become a sea of mud. I stood under a canopy of swaying trees, where the precipitation was a good deal lighter, marveling at the pleasant warmth of my toes, when a foot shot out of nowhere from behind, kicking my legs out from under me. I fell on my face in the wet grass.

I tried to get up, but the foot squashed me back down flat.

"Worms *like* mud," a voice growled, the unmistakable growl of Gabriel Arno. I tried to gasp, but I had no air. Gabriel was stepping on me with his full weight, which was considerable.

"Pull him up," a different voice growled.

I was yanked upright and shoved against a tree. Up close Gabriel's big face looked bigger than ever—the eyes cold and dark and inhuman, and the skin a savage red, ornamented with clusters of pimples, or possibly boils, like something out of the Book of Revelations. Sam Toselli and Jason Barton moved in to flank him, the three forming a tight horseshoe around me. I cast a darting glance over to the muddy path, but the view was obscured, shrouded behind blowing vegetation.

Sam leaned down. "Where do you think you're going, you little freak?"

I opened my mouth to speak, but words had escaped me. I pointed a feeble finger at the parking lot.

"We wanna talk to you first."

"Yeah," Jason spat. "We're not gonna see you again for a while. You know we're getting kicked out of school because of you?"

"Because of me!" I mouthed. The words were there, but my voice had escaped me.

"Because of *you.*" Sam emphasized the word with a poke in my chest. "What's the matter, worm? Nobody to hide behind? No one to protect you?"

"And nowhere to run?" Jason sneered.

Nowhere to run? We were evacuating for Heaven's sake! This was no time for an ambush! I had to make Them see reason. I cleared my throat and found my voice again.

"Look," I ventured reasonably, "why don't we talk this over on the bus. I'll ride next to you, promise! I mean, you guys *did* start the whole thing, but I'm sure we can work something out. I'll put in a good word for you with my dad. You don't want to get in more trouble now, do you?"

Sam seemed to consider this. He cocked his head and stood looking thoughtful, with little rivers of rain streaming down his face.

"Well," he said at last, "we can't really get in *more* trouble, since we're getting kicked out. But yeah, I guess we did start it, now that I think about it." His eyes changed to mean little slits. *"And now we're gonna finish it."*

"Wait!" I wailed reasonably. "It wasn't my fault! I don't see how you can blame me!"

"Oh, Georgette doesn't see! Think we should fix her glasses?"

Sam snatched the lenses from my face and ran backward. The others backed up, too, and soon my glasses were part of a malicious game of toss. I ran in between Them, trying to intercept my eyewear while They cackled with laughter and continued running away, the game driving us deeper into the woods.

At last, Sam held them out, dangling, for me to grab. I started toward him, much relieved, then stopped. He was bending them, twisting them like a pretzel. When both lenses popped out, he flung my broken frames into the wind. I bit my lip, determined not to cry. "You know what Coach Caruso said?" Sam put his face in mine. "He said we should have nailed you when we had the chance. Your time has come, *Worm*."

A pair of hands seized my arms from behind and wrenched them back, as another hand clapped itself over my mouth to stifle my scream. The one over my mouth must have been Gabriel's because it smelled more like a foot than a hand, and a wave of nausea rolled through my interior. I watched Sam wind up, preparing to punch me, then saw him hesitate as if he'd changed his mind.

He had. He bent down to pick up a big stick, and when he straightened up, it was poised in both hands over his shoulder like a baseball bat.

So I did the only thing I could do. I took a deep breath and I held it. I battened down my eyelids. I sucked in my stomach until it hit my spinal column. And then I lost it.

I lost it *completely*.

My muffin, I mean. Abject terror combined with the smell of Gabriel's hand made me spew. Before Sam could deliver his fatal blow, my nutritious bran muffin came shooting out of me like an exploding soft drink.

And the effect was magical. When I opened my eyes, I saw that They'd all leaped away from me—Sam, to get out of the line of fire, and the two behind me, in sympathetic revulsion. A sizable gap had opened between Them, and through that gap I saw the *Road to Freedom*.

Well, I didn't linger. One look at Sam was all it took. There was murder in his eyes and my breakfast all down his front.

I took off running.

26

I RAN THROUGH THE WOODS AS FAST AS I COULD. Through swaying trees and flying sticks, through hailing pinecones and updrafts of pine needles, and when I looked back, They were right on my heels. And They had spread out, an obvious football strategy. I whimpered briefly and picked up my pace, which wasn't easy. Although the overhead foliage had kept the ground fairly dry, the winds had knocked down a lot of branches and tree limbs, and without my glasses, visibility was poor. It was like picking my way through a dark jungle at cheetah-speed, only without cheetah-dexterity, and in consequence, I fell down a lot. But so did They, and because of that, I managed to gain ground.

I had no idea where I was going, not that I could have done anything about it if I had. If you've ever been chased before, specifically, if you've ever been chased by the criminally insane before, you probably noticed that the choice of direction is not really yours. It's Theirs. Particularly when They're spread out like that and one of Them is brandishing a stick. Soon I cleared the trees and reached the top of the big sand dune, with the stormy Delaware Bay below and the rain lashing down hard. The dune was eroding right under my feet. There was hardly any dune grass left at all. The Keep Off sign had blown off into oblivion. In a matter of seconds, I was tumbling down the dune and onto the beach with a painful thud—a painful thud and a heart full of optimism. Because as my body was slipping and sliding and thudding to the bottom, and finally rising up, a five-foot sand sculpture of myself, my quick brain was formulating a plan. I would find the trail that lead from the beach back into the Compound, where I was sure by now help would be waiting.

You see, it never occurred to me that the buses would leave. I pictured search parties already scouring the Cape looking for us—faculty members in tight groups searching high and low, with Mr. Harris in command, overweight, ill-tempered bus drivers honking their horns and cussing freely.

I pictured Mr. Caruso, the guy who'd told Them to nail me, explaining the whole thing to my dad when we got back to school, and in a weird way I was glad this was happening. There could be no opposition to my going to a private school now. None whatsoever.

If I had known the buses would leave without us, I would probably have given up and let the Bruise Brothers catch me. Let Them pulverize me and bury me deep in the sand, a relic for future archaeologists to find.

It was a good thing I *didn't* know. The bay was in a fury, with one huge wave crashing right on top of the next. Probably sounding like thunder, but the howling wind drowned out all other noise. And the beach was a battlefield, pelting me with pebbles and broken shells. I wanted to check if They were gaining on me, but couldn't. I was getting sandblasted. I pulled my jacket over my head and kept my face straight down. The rain was hitting me from all directions, even upward, and there was strange sea life squishing under my feet. I couldn't see what I was treading on, but I could imagine what it was and that only added to my hysteria.

The path to the Compound, I couldn't find it! I looked for it every few seconds, peeling my jacket back just far enough to see out. Even with my glasses on, I would never have found it. I could barely make out the dunes through the sand and rain. Everything looked completely different now. The idea was useless!

And now the gusts were so strong that at times they picked me up and carried me forward. I had to get off the beach soon, before I got swept out to sea! I scanned the dunes again, hoping against hope that I would find the way out, when my eyes fell on the watchtower, that blurry and silent sentinel. Seventy-five feet of steel-reinforced sanctuary. I made for it like a moth zeroing in on a lightbulb.

There was no lock on the tower door, but I still had to fight the wind to get it open, after which I was blown inside as the door slammed shut behind me. I inhaled deep drafts of cool, smelly air, then slowly took in my new surroundings.

My new surroundings were creepy. And the silence was startling. From inside the tower Hurricane Judith sounded like mere background noise. The walls were gray and shadowy. A black spiral staircase grew out of the floor, winding its way to the top like Jack's beanstalk. And I was Jack, only there were *three* giants after me, down on the ground already, somewhere outside the door.

Well, there was no point in going upstairs. I was trapped no matter where I went. I trudged to the opposite wall and sat down to wait for the inevitable. The Bruise Brothers would be here any second. The teachers who were searching for me would find only my mangled carcass.

And I no longer cared. There was sand in my mouth and in my ears. There was sand up my nose and in the corners of my eyes. My new waterproof field-and-stream boots were sopping wet and full of sand. It was hard to tell if my toes were warm or not. I couldn't feel them. I pulled off my boots and slapped them against the wall. Dark gray socks came off next to reveal dark gray feet, gray with sand. I tried brushing them off, but my skin was coming off, too. There were blisters popping up between my toes.

My body hurt. My skin stung. There were broken shells clinging to my jacket and to my burgundy cargo-style pants. Well, they could stay there. My fingers were too raw to pick them off.

I closed my eyes, but not to cry. I didn't have the strength. Instead, I prayed, and though it wasn't the first time I'd prayed this prayer, it was the first time I'd ever prayed it aloud, calling up to Heaven in a voice thick with sincerity.

"Dear God, our most *merciful* Heavenly Father, please crush the Bruise Brothers with Thy mighty hand and save me from Them that persecute me. Crush Sam Toselli, Jason Barton, Gabriel Arno, and, if you have time, Tim Simpson and Drew Lewis—and deliver Them to the place of everlasting fire! Drop Them into the Bottomless Pit in accordance with your wrath, and save he who is deserving, which would be me."

I paused to see if I'd left anything out, and while I was pausing, a disturbing doubt inched its way across my mind like a serpent.

What makes you think you're deserving?

My eyes flew open. Deserving? Of course I was deserving! I shifted uneasily. It was my inner voice speaking, but not my *usual* inner voice, which sounded like my own. This voice was a lot more sinister. A real *nasty* inner voice.

Maybe that's what He's trying to tell you. Maybe this is your punishment, George.

My punishment! I shifted again, even more uneasily. Punishment for what? I racked my brain and came up dry. I'd never done a thing wrong my whole life. My genetic code didn't really allow for it.

Well, it was easy to see what was happening. Exhaustion was making me paranoid, and I was becoming hysterical. I needed to discipline my thoughts, think of something pleasant. Like Mr. Caruso getting fired in front of everybody. Now *that* was a happy thought. Ha! I would enjoy that.

Is everything about you, George? Everything?

What!

You are the biggest jerk that ever lived. All you ever think about is yourself, and that's why everyone hates you!

Now that wasn't true! And why should Anita's voice come back to me, and such a hateful thing to say! Anita had been acting very weird lately. *Probably something to do with hormones* I thought, though I doubted whether she had any yet.

You are the meanest person I've ever met! I hope you wake up one day and find out what you're really like! Because then you'll have nobody! And it'll be too late!

What a thing to say to your best friend! I shook my

head hard. I was becoming unglued. I needed to marshal my thoughts.

I imagined a search party trekking across the beach, a search party following Mr. Harris. I held the picture in my mind, until the words from that secret faculty meeting flooded my brain.

He's obnoxious. Completely obnoxious! Altogether too pleased with himself. Thank God this is his last year!

My head was spinning.

It's a shame he didn't break his neck!

I closed my eyes and clutched my forehead. My mind, usually my most trusted adviser, was unnerving me. I tried envisioning a great search team struggling over the beach with that aging man of science leading the way, his deductive reasoning drawing him closer and closer to the observation tower, knowing that a person of my intellect would surely seek refuge there . . .

Gifted? He's just a pompous snot with a superiority complex!

That voice! That anonymous voice! It belonged to Mr. Harris! The very educator who was out there risking his life to save mine!

Now why would he want to do that? My inner voice chided. *Why would any of them want to do that? They all hate you, George, with the possible exception of Mr. Zimmerman, but he doesn't count. This is their chance to get rid of you forever, and a chance like this doesn't come along twice!*

"Shut up!" I told the Voice. "I'm not listening anymore!" I covered my ears, which didn't help, of course, since the noise was inside my head.

They left you here! You're all alone!

"No, I'm not!" I wailed. "They *have* to be looking for

me, if only for reasons of liability! They would never leave me behind!"

Then where are the Bruise Brothers? Why aren't They here yet?

The Voice had a point there. My mind started racing. The Bruise Brothers should have been here by now, that is, if They'd actually chased me down the beach at all. I tried to remember when I'd last turned to look at Them. It had been on top of the dune right before I'd gone over the edge.

They turned around, George! The Voice giggled, menacingly. *They ran back through the woods and hopped on a bus!*

"That's not true!"

They're on Their way home now, and you're out here all by yourself!

"That can't be true!"

And you're going to die out here!

I sat up straight, staring in horror. Then I sagged back down, my rebuttal lost on my lips. It *was* true. The Voice was right.

Hot tears stabbed the corners of my eyes. "I'm all alone!" I sobbed. "And I'm going to die out here!"

I pressed my face to the wall and let misery wash the sand from my cheeks. I cried and I cried, harder than I'd cried in years.

And I did so for a very long time.

27

I MOPPED MY FACE WITH A SANDY SLEEVE AND told myself to snap out of it. There was no point in feeling sorry for myself. Not yet, anyway, because I might be wrong. There might be people searching for me. It wouldn't hurt to take a look and see. And I wouldn't have to go outside. There were viewing ports upstairs.

I climbed the staircase and found the viewing ports—four slits cut in the tower wall. Each blast of wind sent the rain shooting in like a fire hose. I ran to one in between blasts and saw a thick fog of swirling sand with a *green* sky above it—a dark, sickly sky, a bilious sky, and no signs of life below. Life couldn't have survived out there. I jumped aside before the next squall could spray me, then descended a couple of steps and sat down.

There was no doubt about it. The Bruise Brothers were heading home and I was in here being punished by God.

I would never go home again!

Home! A vision appeared in my mind's eye. Our

modest but lovely four-bedroom Colonial, nineteen hundred and eighty-six square feet of insulated comfort. I remembered arguing vehemently in favor of the new foam insulation over the old fiberglass-batt kind but having to concede to my parents' cost-cutting efforts. Funny how it didn't seem important anymore! The aluminum siding that I had picked out. Our neatly manicured lawn. The birdbath that wild horses couldn't drag me near because it contained a myriad of pathogens.

I thought of my mom on the front walk waiting for me to come home, a hand held to her heart in breathless anticipation, standing between two carefully clipped rows of assorted flowering shrubs. The dog was with her, our lovable Irish setter—the sunshine bouncing off his silky mahogany coat—waiting for me, too, and smiling visibly the way only happy dogs do.

Tears rolled down my cheeks.

Not that we ever *had* a dog, but nostalgia was stealing over me, and, I don't know, he seemed to balance out the picture somehow.

I sighed.

My poor mom. She'd be beside herself when she found out I was dead. She'd put up such a brave front—acting so cheerful—actually *singing* as she'd packed my camping gear. My tired mom. Taking care of me was her life's work. Was she tired because of me? Yes, she was tired because of me. I saw that now. And what had I ever done for her? Not much. An autographed photo of myself every Mother's Day. That wasn't much. Or at least, not nearly enough. I wished I could make it up to her, or even just say thank you for once.

And my dad. I wished I could thank him, too, for all sorts of stuff I couldn't even think of. I would thank him for "things too numerous to mention." And all the speeches. He *loved* giving me speeches. Like on Monday morning, "Mark my words, George, when you come back on Friday, you will not be the same boy who left." Well, he was right in a way because by Friday I would be dead. Or even sooner. The human body dehydrates in what? Three to five days? It would be less for me. I had less of a body.

My mouth felt suddenly dry. I licked my lips, getting a fresh coating of sand on my tongue.

The wind was really loud, constant now, no longer coming in gusts. I palmed my ears the way I did as a kid whenever my dad started lecturing me. I stopped doing that as I got older because I saw how rude it was, and because it really pissed him off. These days I hummed to myself whenever he got started.

He was always giving me advice, convinced that I was listening. Trying to get me to make friends, that was his big thing.

"If you give others a chance, George, they'll give you a chance."

I always wondered, *a chance to do what? Hit me first?*

"You have to *be* a friend if you want to *have* a friend." He was always saying that, even though he knew all I cared about was becoming a scientist. One day I'd make a name for myself and gain people's respect. I'd become one of the world's top minds—a great man.

"Son, I think a great man needs to have more than a great mind. It's not who he is but what he does that makes a man great, and for that he needs a great *heart*." I'd dismissed this as pointless backchat at the time . . . but it made sense now. My dad was saying I didn't have a great heart. That I was a completely heartless person. A heartless jerk.

The biggest jerk that ever lived. What good was having a superior brain if you had an inferior heart?

Now, Anita had a great heart, but nobody liked her either. *Probably because she hangs around me,* I thought bitterly. I remembered the day she showed up wearing her new black aviator jacket. At the time I'd accused her of coveting mine. Now I could see she'd only bought it so that I wouldn't get made fun of alone. She was always taking care of me—like getting in line in the cafeteria to buy strawberry milk for me day after day so that I wouldn't have to pass Their table and get heckled, getting heckled herself and acting like she didn't mind.

And getting beaten up in the woods for me. She'd been a scapegoat, taken my punishment, just like Sydney Carton in my book. Not a *willing* scapegoat, but a scapegoat nonetheless. A true-blue friend. The very truest and the very bluest. No wonder God was punishing me. I'd never done a thing for her!

But if I lived through this, I'd become the best friend she ever had! I would make it up to her, and everyone else!

And Sam! After what I'd done to him! Watching him work on his Junior Scientist project, knowing he wasn't doing it right and enjoying his embarrassment! No wonder he'd chased me to my death! Who could've blamed him for that? Why, I would have done no less! I would make it up to him, too, if I lived through this.

I sank to my knees. "God!" I cried. "I take all that other stuff back! I didn't mean any of it! I want You to know that I'm sorry for being a jerk my whole life, and if You let me live, I'll make it up to everybody. I swear I'll be different! I'll be kind and considerate to everyone whether they deserve it or not! Please give me another chance! I promise to help my fellow man! I promise to—"

I broke off here because a loud rattling sound below made me bolt to my feet and nearly bite off my tongue. I ran downstairs and leaned over the rail. It was the door shaking in its frame. Up and down and side to side, as if a jackhammer were against it hammering away. And like an idiot I stood rooted to the spot, hypnotized, the painful popping in my ears telling me that the air pressure was falling fast.

A split second later there was a punch. The door was gone! The outside world had become a huge suction pump!

Escape seemed impossible, but I somehow managed to jump backward and fly straight up the steps in a flash, as if I'd sprouted the wings of an eagle. I came to a halt, however, in the next moment, after tripping over my feet and falling headlong into the rigid embrace of the winding steel steps.

After that, I was out cold.

28

I AWOKE TO THE SOUND OF SPLASHING WATER. I lay peacefully listening to the gentle sloshing until I felt the pain in my forehead, and as soon as I felt it, it became huge and hot and blinding. I touched the spot, felt a sharp sting, and my eyes popped open. A small scream escaped my lips. My fingers were covered in blood. Suddenly the tower walls seemed to spin about me. I took off my jacket, held the fuzzy collar against the wound with shaking hands, and realized that I couldn't hear the hurricane anymore. I needed to see outside.

I forced my wobbly legs up the stairs until I reached the viewing ports, and as I looked out, I couldn't believe my eyes—searing sunlight in a powder blue sky, what Heaven must look like to the dearly departed, and glittering blue-gray water below, alive with feasting seagulls diving and scrambling for their catch! I laughed out loud.

"God! You let me live! You gave me another chance! A chance to turn over a new leaf! And I swear I'll do all the things I promised! I'll make it up to everybody! I will help my fellow man! I will put myself last while putting others first, and I shall act like I don't mind doing it!"

Then I looked down. I stopped laughing.

"God?" I called. "Where's the beach?"

For the beach was gone. The tower was standing in the Delaware Bay.

Okay, I thought, *I'm not going to panic. I'm going to assess the situation from all angles, then I'll panic.* I proceeded up the stairs to the rooftop, where I caught my breath. I could see for miles—the blurry pine forest, the blurry campground, what was left of the blurry dunes. It was a wasteland! And the parking lot. A lump grew in my throat. It was a lake now. And just as I'd suspected. No buses. Only the Music Man's pickup truck alone in the water. He'd probably hopped on a bus with the rest of them, afraid to drive in the storm. Afraid to get caught in a hurricane again.

And I could see why!

I leaned on the guardrail, inadvertently ripping the fuzzy collar off my cut. But I was too depressed to notice the excruciating pain this caused because I had just turned to look farther inland.

Which wasn't the right word at all. I was looking at swampland, tons of fallen trees, hacked apart and leaning over in the flowing floodwater. And there was camp! The bunkhouses, the latrines, the mess hall—all in water up to their rooflines. But they'd be all right. They were built to last. The newer building, however, the Administrative Office slash Nurse's Quarters, that was finished. It was like looking down at a dollhouse with the roof off. The first floor was almost completely submerged, the second a catastrophe of exposed beams, wall studs, and broken junk—

the whole building leaning up against a tree, tilting east toward the bay.

I peered west at the horizon, caught a flicker of movement beyond the forest. Vehicles moving? I squinted harder. Emergency vehicles? I couldn't tell, but no one coming into Cape Rose State Park. Why should they? The park had evacuated as scheduled, and I probably hadn't been reported missing yet. From the position of the sun, I calculated the time at roughly two fifteen or two twenty. I doubted the rest of the class had reached school, with a zillion coastal residents heading for high ground at the same time. Eventually they'd realize I'd gotten left behind and send for help, but who knew when that would be? It might be hours from now.

Hours and hours with nothing to drink, and I was so thirsty now I could hardly stand it. And, contrary to that, I had to pee, and the latrines were a hundred yards away and at the bottom of the sea.

My cut throbbed with new vigor. I laid my head to rest on the rail and stood looking down, lost in thought, staring dully at the pale concrete between my feet and trying to ignore the rude, incessant chatter of the many happy seagulls scavenging the bay, when I became aware of another sound. The sound of a voice. Not my *inner* voice this time, which I hoped I'd never hear from again, but a human voice. For a second I thought I'd imagined it. I strained to listen. There it was again, coming from the campground. What was it saying?

I scanned the buildings, my foggy vision resting on the second floor of the torn-up Administrative Office slash Nurse's Quarters. It must have come from there, although

I couldn't detect a living soul among the rubbish. But maybe the person could see me.

"Ahoy there!" I shouted, jumping up and down and twirling my jacket around in a big circle over my head. "What did you say? I didn't quite catch it!"

I froze and listened intently. The response was faint, but the words were clear.

"Help! Somebody! Help!"

I recognized the speaker right away.

It was Sam Toselli.

29

SO, THE BRUISE BROTHERS WERE HERE! I wasn't alone! And though I was still racked by thirst and a savage desire to pee . . . why, They probably were, too! There was comfort in that.

Then I got suspicious. I yelled, "I can't see you! Can you see me?" and nobody answered. *Is this a trap?* I wondered. *Are They luring me down there so They can finish me off and make it look like an accident?* A legitimate concern for a guy who'd recently been on the wrong end of a homicidal manhunt through the forest, but entirely unfounded. Because a moment later I heard a plaintive "Help! Please!" and there was anguish in Sam's voice. Genuine anguish. I was sure of it because there was often genuine anguish in my own voice, and I could easily spot a fake.

So the Bruise Brothers needed help. But what could I do? I needed help, too!

Then it hit me. It hit me like a tightly packed snowball to the back of the head. This was my chance to help my fellow man. I'd promised God that I would make it up to everybody, and He'd taken me seriously. He had let me live. It was too late to take it back now. God and I had a deal going.

I had seen the light.

And not only the light but the flashing *bar lights* atop two or three emergency vehicles turning off the distant roadway at a slow crawl toward Cape Rose—a rescue crew in progress! Not exactly the Coast Guard coming, but that wasn't important. Anyone with an inflatable dinghy would do. The *important* thing was . . . the Bruise Brothers wouldn't know help was coming. So I had to act fast! I had to go and administer help in all kinds of heroic ways before the rescue crew reached Them. And They'd be amazed by my calm and my sense of leadership. When word of this spread, possibly making *Good Morning, America* if I played my cards right, people would form lines just to shake my hand. No one would ever utter the words "pompous snot" in reference to me again!

"STAY WHERE YOU ARE! I'LL BE RIGHT THERE!" I bellowed, studying the water. Well, I would have to swim. A bit of a problem, since I didn't know how. I could manage a rude doggy paddle if pressed, but that was it, and even then I resembled a nervous Chihuahua having a series of uncontrollable spasms.

Still, the water looked calm. It might not be too difficult to cross. The real problem, I learned after hopping down the steps, would be finding the way out. The tower had filled like a well. I couldn't see the doorway. I would have to dive down and find it. Trembling, I gripped the handrails. The thought of submerging my head simply terrified me. It had kept my hair dry since I was a child.

If it hadn't been for the Music Man, or rather, if it

hadn't been for the Music Man's high-pitched voice coming back to haunt me, I might be standing there still.

Face your fears, George. Face your fears.

"Okay," I said, swallowing hard. "Just a minute."

Seize fate by the throat, George!

I dipped a toe in the water. "I'll be right with you."

You remind me of myself at your age.

"I'm going! I'm going!"

It was the kick in the pants I needed. Determination seeped back into my system. I let go of the railing, tied my jacket around my hips for a little added buoyancy, then dropped for a couple of deep knee bends. I took a long breath, pinched my nose shut, and plunged down into ice water. Then I bobbed back up and climbed the steps. This was not going to be easy.

I repeated the process, adding an expert donkey kick off the stairs to my routine, and as I shot through the water my hand brushed the splintered doorway. I had found the way out! So now the hard part was over. I torpedoed myself through the opening and rose to the sparkling surface of the bay, where I discovered immediately that I had been wrong. *Very* wrong.

Wrong about the hard part being over, for when I say I "rose to the sparkling surface of the bay," what I mean is "my butt rose to the sparkling surface of the bay," and I had one heck of a time getting my head out of the water. You see, the current had me in its grip, and instead of assuming the dog-paddle position right away, as was my plan, I adopted the clumsy, thrashing stroke that even the hardiest swimmers tend to fall back on when they are drowning.

A sad ending to my story.

Or so I thought.

I WAS GOING DOWN FOR THE UMPTEENTH TIME and was just about to lose all hope entirely, when divine intervention, in the form of a floating tree branch, came along and conked me on the ear in such a way as to tell me that all was not lost. A little spooky, but there it was. God must have been keeping an eye on me.

I lassoed the branch with flailing arms and attached my upper half to it like Velcro, and now even the floodwater seemed to be on my side, flowing right into the Compound. With my outstretched arm providing the rudder and the occasional kicking motion making me feel as if I were doing something more than just not thinking about what might be swimming underneath me, I let the current carry me all the way into camp.

Well, me and a whole lot of other stuff polluting the water. Driftwood and trash, aluminum cans, bits of cloth and broken glass.

I wondered how long it might take the rescuers to

reach us. An hour, maybe? Who knew? It might be a long and thirsty wait. But at least I no longer had to pee.

I blushed at the thought as I pictured the upcoming scene in my mind.

The Bruise Brothers standing there, eyes big as petri dishes, mouths hanging open in wonder, gaping at me as I floated in. I would screw up my face to better depict my pain and suffering, and start paddling hard through the water. Then Sam and Jason would lean out of the window . . . No, *Sam* would lean out and haul me aboard, and then we'd gaze at each other the way we'd done so many times in the past, only without all of the hatred on his part and all of the fear on mine. We'd goggle at each other with *respect,* and it would be a pleasant change.

A very pleasant change.

But it didn't work out that way. When I paddled hard up to the building, the window was empty, and the place, sagging heavily against the tree, looked as if it had been bombed—the glass blown out of the windows, the roof nearly gone, and that big red Welcome to Cape Rose banner caught in the branches of the tree, fluttering noisily against a broken wall. It all looked so eerie, and so deserted.

"Hello?" I called. "Is anybody there?"

Utter silence. I cruised up to a window and grabbed hold.

"Hello?"

Mounting the sill, a difficult maneuver with the current tugging me away, I stumbled onto the sloping floor and stood up shivering in the breeze. I thought, *If this is a trick . . .*

"George."

It was Sam's voice, but it sounded odd, kind of muffled.

"Where are you guys?" I asked.

"Over here."

I looked about me, and my heart started pounding. The chairs, the filing cabinets, all of the office furniture had cascaded downhill into a heap against the lower wall, the very place where his voice had come from. *Sam was buried alive.* I made my way over and saw the back of his head on the thin brown carpeting. Covering him were large planks of wood, the remains of a desk. On top of that lay a heavy aluminum shelf unit, pinning Sam down.

I knelt beside him.

"Sam! Oh, my God! Are you okay?"

His head turned. I saw his profile, and the ghost of a grin.

"Took you long enough."

My heart skipped a beat. "You're okay, then?"

"I don't know."

"Are you in pain?"

"Nope. Not like I was. I think my legs went to sleep. I can't feel a thing anymore."

"Well, no wonder!" I cried. "With all this weight on you!" I attempted to lift up the shelf unit, but it didn't budge. I sat back on my heels.

"I'm going to need a hand with this. Where are the others?"

He let out a cheerless laugh. "Home, probably. They turned around and went back through the woods. Said I was taking it too far, that I was outta my mind. And they were right. Sorry, George. I never should've done that. I don't know what was wrong with me. All I kept thinking about was what my parents would do when they heard I got kicked out of school. It's good you can run fast."

"I was highly motivated."

"I never saw anybody run that fast before. Coach Caruso should've been there."

"Coach Caruso's the one who told you to nail me, remember?"

"No, he didn't. I made that up. I was trying to scare you. C'mon, you didn't believe that, did you?"

"Believe it?" I smiled broadly. "Do I look that stupid?" We shared a chuckle. The relief on hearing this piece of good news was overwhelming. It's distressing to think your gym teacher has targeted you for a mob-style slaying on a mandatory class trip. There's something very unsportsmanlike about it.

But *this* was nice. A subdued Sam Toselli lying there, full of remorse and looking up at me, and me brimming over with the milk of human kindness, the two of us discussing our checkered past amicably. It was very nice. And studying his face, I was struck by just how young it seemed. Young and innocent. Maybe because all of the meanness had drained out of it. All of the color, too. It was a very pale, innocent face.

He turned a bit more my way and his eyes grew suddenly large.

"God, you're all beat up! There's a big friggin' gash going from one side of your head to the other. What'd you do to yourself?"

"You don't want to know," I said mysteriously. "Believe me, things got pretty rough out there. Friggin' rough, in fact."

"That's gotta hurt *bad*."

"*Bad*," I said, "hardly meets the description. It's friggin' *agony*," and from the way he nodded, I could tell he'd grasped my meaning perfectly. But it was really a lie because I couldn't feel it anymore. Saltwater makes a wonderful analgesic.

We regarded each other quietly, respectfully you might say, for several moments before Sam observed, "You know what? You're a real good friend to me, George. A real good friend." And believe it or not, when he said this, the whole room seemed to light up just like a Christmas tree. The broken glass started twinkling, the miscellaneous office crap became vivid and colorful, and the heavy metal shelves pinning Sam down seemed to shine like polished silver. And the thought crossed my mind that this whole terrifying ordeal, even the two terrifying years of torture that preceded it, might have been well worth it just to hear those words from Sam Toselli.

I grinned at him the way a real good friend would, and I'm not ashamed to say my eyes felt more than a little humid. I blinked them dry. Sam grinned back at me, then drew a breath and closed his eyes.

"The best worm I ever had."

He inhaled again, a quick shallow breath, and I stared at him in alarm. The words had come out thick and slurred. I touched his forehead. It was cold and clammy.

"Yup . . . a good worm." He was panting now, and staring blankly. His eyes were glazed, the pupils dilated. He wasn't okay. He was anything *but* okay.

He's going into shock! I realized. A second after I realized this, I sprang into action, hardly knowing what I was doing. A rush of adrenaline sent me vaulting to my knees, and another rush, empowering me with what felt like the strength of ten, enabled me to send the shelf unit tumbling off of Sam's body. I snatched up each piece of the broken desk, tossing heavy planks over my shoulder like so many Lincoln Logs, then steeled myself to view the carnage: a pair of legs so twisted and bent, so crooked and fixed that they looked more like the limbs of a mangled action figure than the legs of an eighth-grade kid.

31

SAM BABBLED WHILE I WORKED, OBLIVIOUS to the fear that gripped me now from head to toe. I had never been so frightened in all my life, *especially for a person who didn't happen to be me.*

"You know what, George?" he mused. "I don't wanna go home."

"Sure you do, Sam." My voice trembled. I wanted to cover him with something warm, but there was nothing as far as a blanket in the room. The Cape Rose banner would do no good, it was made of thin nylon, and my jacket was soaking wet.

"No, I don't. They're gonna kill me when they find out what happened. I can't go home."

"They're not going to kill you. They're not going to kill anyone." I swallowed twice to steady my voice. "I'll tell everyone it was my fault. Everything that happened, and I'll make them believe me. Adults *always* believe me. Don't you worry about a thing."

I had to think. *Do I elevate his legs? I would have to*

immobilize them first. Or do I wait for help? Where is that rescue team? Why are they taking so long!

"You'd do that for me?"

"Yes, of course, I would, and you would do it for me." I had to do *something* for him. I scanned the room, and my eyes lit on a few scattered pieces of wall paneling. I fetched one, a nice wide one, wide enough to brace Sam's legs in their unnatural positions and plenty long enough to support his head and back, as well. I brought it down to where he lay.

He was still rambling, choppy words between shallow breaths. "I dunno if I'd do it for you. No, I don't think I would. You're better than me. You're better than everybody."

"No, I'm not," I said, sliding the panel underneath him. The drawers of the desk were half-buried in the wreckage, their contents spilled on the floor, among which was a roll of heavy tape. I began a sloppy job of binding Sam's hips and legs to the panel with the tape, trying to make a splint, *praying* that I was doing it right. Why hadn't I learned first aid? "I'm not better than anybody. You're talking to the *worm*, remember?"

This got a laugh out of him, a drunken laugh. I ripped the tape with my teeth and patted the end in place. He was still laughing.

"Now listen, Sam." I cradled his face. "You're hurt. You're hurt bad. *Friggin' bad,* and I don't want you to move. Help is coming. I saw a rescue team from the top of the tower, but they might not get here for a while. Can you keep still for me until help comes?"

"George," he said, his voice a cracked whisper, "I don't think I *can* move."

"That's fine," I nodded, "that's a good thing right now!"

I picked up his hand and squeezed it. "We'll stay here together and wait, and any minute now help will come. Everything is going to be okay. Nothing bad is going to happen, because I won't let it!"

But even as I said this, I knew it wasn't true, for at that very moment the building produced a huge shudder. It wobbled back and forth, the framework creaking like an old rocking chair, before it sagged even more against the tree.

The building was going to fall.

32

I HAD TO STAY CALM. ANY MINUTE NOW THE walls would fold in on us like a house of cards and we would be crushed, but I had to stay calm. Somewhere deep in my mind I realized that I could always save myself. I could always jump into the sea and take my chances. But somewhere even *deeper* in my mind, I knew that that was wrong. Without me Sam had no chance. I would never leave him.

"Sam," I said, turning to him calmly, "we've got to get out of here!"

His eyes were closed. "But I like it here."

God, I thought, *he's delirious!* "You need to stay awake now. Pay attention!" I gave his face a little shake. "I'm going to try to make a raft." I looked frantically about me. "But I have no idea how."

"George, you're the smartest guy at school. The whole world, probably. You'll figure it out."

Okay, I thought, *maybe he's not so delirious.* There

seemed to be only one possibility, namely a long, rectangular folding table anchored against the high wall. I dragged the table over, wondering how I would ever manage to get Sam onto the thing, and then wondering how on earth I would lower him into the water without hurting him, when I dropped it top down on the carpet and saw that I needn't have worried at all. The table had a crack in it! It wouldn't have floated for two seconds!

"Why can't you be more like George?" crooned Sam, in a sleepy, singsong voice. "George never flunked Beginner Finger Painting."

Beginner Finger Painting? I couldn't remember having taken that course.

"Sam!" I said sharply, "Stop babbling!"

Like a maniac, I began rooting through the junk pile, looking for something, anything, we could use for a raft, but there was nothing!

"God!" I buried my face in my hands. "I'm trying! Can't You see that I'm trying? I know all this is my fault! All because of that stupid Junior Scientist fair. I could've helped Sam then, but I didn't because I was a jerk, and now look. He's going to die! And it doesn't matter that I'm not a jerk anymore. It's too late!"

"George," Sam breathed, "stop babbling."

"It's not like Bernoulli's principle is even used anymore!" I shouted up to Heaven. "It's obsolete! It's friggin' obsolete now!" I looked around the devastated room again, my gaze landing on the fluttering red welcome banner. I shook my head sadly, stooping beside Sam, tears streaming down my face. "You know where you went wrong? You forgot that air resistance is proportional to velocity. I could have told you that! If I hadn't been such a jerk, I would have told you that, and you wouldn't be dying now! I have only myself to blame, only myself!"

I ignored Sam's bewildered stare and continued to brood on the subject, vaguely drumming my fingers on his buzzed head and weeping quietly at the hideous banner. The hideous blood red banner with its words billowing out just to mock us. Just to mock *me*. Welcome to Cape Rose. Welcome? It should have read Cape Rose: Enter at Your Peril for what it was worth!

And then I gasped. I felt my mouth flop open. I felt my eyes fairly leap from their sockets as I gawked at the banner, at the big beautiful Cape Rose red banner—the merry pennant that had been billowing outward the whole time just to mock us. Because now it was billowing upward, and it was curling up high enough to allow me a full, uninterrupted view of the watchtower in the distance, and of the pair of blurry yellow objects at its bottom.

"They're here!" I cried. "The boats! The boats are here! We're going to be rescued!" I whooped with joy and sprang lightly to my feet, hurdling Sam's inert body so that I could climb the broken wall and tug the banner out of the tree. "See? I told you I wouldn't let anything bad happen! I'm just going to flag them down now."

I wrenched the bright fabric free of the tree and flapped it hard above my head, shouting at the top of my voice. I danced wildly around and around, and I jumped high up and down, flapping and shouting all the while, until disaster, which I'd felt sure had finally quit looming and taken its evil business elsewhere, decided to strike.

33

MOVING ABOUT SO VIOLENTLY IN MY FLAG-ging-down efforts, I wasn't aware of how much the room had begun trembling again. It was the sound of a sharp crack, as loud as a gunshot, followed by a prolonged creaking, as of a hundred rusty gates swinging open one by one, that made me stop jumping and drop the banner.

Events took on a nightmarish quality. The floor started buckling, first in one spot, then in another. Floorboards came ripping through the thin brown carpeting. A ragged hole started forming near Sam, leaving me no time to think. If I had had time to think, I would have thought that with the walls about to cave in on us, there was not a blessed thing I could have done to keep us from getting killed. Instead, I scuttled thoughtlessly around the hole and spread myself over Sam, a skinny human shield, with my arms stretching the width of his wall-panel splint, my hands gripping the edges and my cheek squashing tight against his. I was stretching and gripping and squashing him so tightly that when we fell through the floor to the water below, we fell as one body, with a hard and heavy slap. Then we plunged underwater.

Seconds later we plunged right back up. We rocked and dipped on the surface, and then the current jerked us and we drifted out into bright sunlight. It would have amazed me to find I had wasted so much time searching for what I had already taped Sam to, the perfect raft, if I hadn't already been amazed we weren't smashed to smithereens. Crashing noises told me that the walls were falling down. We'd drifted safely out of range of the walls, but not far enough to avoid getting hit by the air strike. Pieces of broken glass and fragments of the building were hitting me like hailstones.

Then everything got quiet, strangely quiet. There was nothing to hear except the sound of waves lapping and the soothing hum of two motorboats coming in closer. There was nothing to hear of Sam. He was strangely quiet. I put my ear to his lips. He wasn't breathing.

"Breathe!" I yelled. "Sam, please breathe!"

"I can't," he sputtered. He coughed several times. "You're . . . squeezing . . . my . . . chest."

I rolled a little to one side, overcome with relief. He was alive! Sam Toselli was alive, and it was because of me! I could have left him. I could have chosen to save myself and simply left him there to die, but I didn't. Instead, I seized fate by the throat and put my life on the line, and I saved him!

I told him all this, adding, "but you don't have to thank me, because that's what friends are for. I know I let you down once, back when I was a jerk, but I want you to know that I will never let you down again. No matter what. We're going to be friends for life now. It'll be George and

Sam forever. Through thick and thin, through fair weather and foul, and till death us do part. This," I declared, so near to him that our eyeballs were almost touching, "is my solemn promise."

Sam did not reply immediately. He must have been moved by my words. Then he let out a groan, a long, deep groan of contentment, louder than the droning of the nearby motorboats, and settled back peacefully on our raft to wait for help to arrive.

34

THE RESCUE MEN, THREE STRAPPING EMERgency medical technicians with Cape Rose Volunteer Fire Department across the backs of their orange coats, plucked us out of the sea. As I watched the men in Sam's boat minister to his injuries I found that I was suffering the same sort of pangs a new mother must feel on handing her baby over to a teenage sitter for the first time. I felt . . . protective, like Sam still needed me to look after him. I was afraid to take my eyes off him. Afraid to let him go.

"You did that?"

I whirled around to the voice behind me and nearly tipped my boat. A big, strapping specimen of a fellow with Viking-length hair braced me with a burly arm.

"You put that splint on him? You must be one special kid."

"It wasn't hard to do," I told him honestly. "I'm sure anyone could have done it." All I did was stop thinking about myself and start thinking about someone else. I would have to remember that in the future.

He shook his head, whistling softly. "Son, you must be in terrible pain right now."

Pain? He must have meant my cut. "Oh, that's just a flesh wound. It doesn't even hurt anymore." Naturally my hand flew to the spot to investigate, and I was rewarded with a burning pain that shot straight through my skull. The man took a thick wad of white gauze from a metal box marked First Aid. He applied it to my head, saying, "Hold it like this, with your fingers flat, and keep pressing on it."

We headed off, following Sam's boat, which was already cruising through the Compound at a fast clip.

"Your teacher'll be glad we found you," the Viking continued over his shoulder from his position at the helm. "He's been crazy with worry, and driving everybody else crazy, too."

I sat up tall, forcing my thoughts away from the roar in my head. "My teacher?"

"Short man, not a lot of hair. Said he was your music teacher."

"MR. ZIMMERMAN!"

"Right, Mr. Zimmerman. We picked him up a little while ago. That's how we knew you were out here."

"Picked him up? Picked him up where?"

"About a half-mile up the coast."

I was stunned. "What was he doing there?"

"Looking for you, from what I heard. You were on a class trip that had to evacuate, right? And your friend and you got lost? Well, Mr. Zimmerman volunteered, no, he insisted on staying behind and rounding you boys up so he could bring you home in his truck, but then the storm overtook him. Chopper spotted him up the coast hanging onto some sort of homemade surfboard."

I was speechless. Mr. Zimmerman had stayed behind to rescue us? He'd insisted on combing the Cape himself, thereby jeopardizing his own safety instead of putting the task in the more capable hands of trained professionals, just to save our skins? My God! The man was not only stout, he was stouthearted! I needed to tell him that!

"Where is he?" I cried. "I've got to see him!"

We were navigating through the forest, an obstacle course of downed trees and power lines. A siren wailed in the distance, Sam's ambulance on its way.

"No," the man hollered, "don't take that off! Keep putting pressure on it!"

In my excitement I'd let the gauze slip away from my head. I picked it up. Then I dropped it immediately because it was dripping with my blood, a dark, sticky, nauseating sight that set off a roar in my stomach bigger than the one I'd felt in my head. I saw the Viking's arm fly out to catch me as I swayed in my seat, but it was too late. I keeled over, toppling onto the floor of the boat in a dead faint.

And until I was safely installed in my own ambulance, with siren blaring and a heavy-duty painkiller inserted in my arm, I stayed keeled.

35

YES, I WAS HURT, BUT COMPARED WITH SAM my injuries were few and trifling. A three-and-a-half-inch crevice splitting my forehead in two, which required thirty-six stitches to close! But I had very little pain to speak of, thanks to the miracles of modern medicine.

I stayed in the hospital for three days, mostly for observation, and Sam for three weeks, during which time he underwent surgery and began a lengthy term of intense orthopedic care. But his prognosis was encouraging. No football in the near future, of course, but perhaps in the distant future if everything went well. I know holding on to that hope got him through some very long days.

It felt strange being without him. I thought about him constantly during my stay in the hospital except, of course, when I was receiving visitors, which by early evening of the first day, I seemed to be receiving nothing but.

They were the usual suspects. My dear, wonderful mother, just as wonderfully choked up and fretful as was nice to see. And my dear dad. My dear, hearty dad. Only not so very hearty these days. He was a sad dad, sad he'd ever let me go on the trip to Cape Rose, blaming himself, as if he should have known instinctively the danger I was about to face. So it fell to me to cheer him up. I let him know his parting words of wisdom had come true, that I was decidedly *not* the same boy who'd left Conrad T. Parks Middle School on Monday morning and that I *had* learned a thing or two. Actually three things, as I counted them.

The first from Mrs. Love. A lesson called Get All the Facts Before You Leap to Conclusions.

A mixed bag of teachers had arrived en masse to take turns gushing over me, and you can readily imagine how standoffish I was with the not-so-Love-ing lady when she perched on my bedside and peered at me through tearstained bifocals. I allowed her to press my hand, holding in my resentment, just barely, but when she said, "Oh, George, what a hero you are! And I'd always thought of you as, shall we say . . . delicate?" I opened the hatch and dropped the bomb.

"I can't imagine why. I'm usually thought of as a pompous snot with a superiority complex."

Mrs. Love lurched. "Where did you hear that?"

"I have my sources," I said, smiling. "My agents, you know, are everywhere. But not to worry." I patted her hand. "I'm letting bygones be bygones." It was really the only way.

"You must have overheard us talking! But we weren't talking about you, George. We would *never* talk about you that way." She lowered her voice. "I'm afraid we were talking about . . . Mr. Zimmerman."

"MR. ZIMMERMAN!" I cried. My face froze in an expression of joy.

"*Shhh*. The day he tripped over you and fell. I'm

ashamed to admit it, but we were talking about him. Frankly, we've never cared for him very much. He'd always acted so superior, as if he were better than us. But now he seems quite the opposite! Warm and kind and friendly. Such a wonderful sense of humor. You must have brought out the best in him, George!"

"MR. ZIMMERMAN!" I cried again, still frozen in my joy.

"Yes," said Mrs. Love, shushing me with a finger on my lips, "and it's sad to think he'll be leaving us at the end of the year, taking back his old job in New York. It seems the school fell apart when he left. He's a very gifted music teacher, you know. And now that he's warmed up the way he has, well, I know we're all going to miss him."

I had to agree with her there. Mr. Zimmerman had become so warm that people were calling him Mr. Sunshine for the way he bounced in and out of my room and up and down the hospital corridors, recounting his adventure to anyone who would listen—his death-defying experience curled up in a fetal position on the floor of his truck as he rode out his second hurricane, and his subsequent rescue mission, hanging on to his wooden submarine-tank and sailing straight up the coast. His tale held us spellbound for hours, which tickled him to no end, and he spent entire days shaking hands with every nurse and orderly he could stop, and accepting, gleefully, the numerous high fives bestowed on him by members of the custodial staff.

But he deserved it all, and more. For even though I would be crowned the "Hero of Conrad T. Parks Middle School," what with the publicity and the fanfare, the T-shirts bearing my likeness, and the parade that would be given in my honor, *Mr. Zimmerman would always be my hero*. He'd risked his life to save mine because he'd cared about me, cared even though I'd never given him a good reason *to* care. And if I reminded him even a little of himself at my age, well, that was okay by me. I would be proud of that.

As proud as I was to call him my friend.

The second thing I learned came to me quite suddenly. Out of the blue, you might say. Yet somehow it seemed I'd known it all along without really knowing it. It's hard to see a thing clearly when it's there in front of you all the time. This doesn't make much sense, but it's true.

Before Anita walked into the room, I was aware of how much I missed her, but when she sat on the edge of my bed, laughing, "You are the biggest jerk that ever lived!" all over me, her green eyes all wet and shiny, I saw just how lovely she was. How really, really lovely she was. And I couldn't stop myself. I just had to tell her.

"You know what, Anita? You happen to be a very beautiful girl."

Words I never thought I'd say aloud, let alone on the printed page, but I'm glad that I said them. Anita's eyes lit up like a couple of firecrackers.

And then I discovered something else. That I'd been wrong. Totally wrong in what I'd said before because Anita *did* have hormones, great seething masses of them, and they were pressing me now in a rib-crushing moment of unrestrained joy. Unrestrained joy on her side, suffocating, hair-swallowing panic on mine. But in a way it was nice, so I let her squeeze me for a bit.

Then all it took was a simple, "Ow! Get off me!" to return us to our points of origin, me lying and her hovering. I adjusted my hospital gown and beamed at her.

"I really meant what I said," I told her. "And I'll go even

further. *You're the most beautiful girl in the world.* Unless, of course," I gave her a wink, "it's just the pain medicine talking." Which made Anita giggle and beam right back at me.

I gave my IV drip a little pat.

And then I learned the most important thing of all—that I was *gifted*. Gifted in the deepest and truest sense of the word. Because a friend like Anita was the greatest gift I could ever have. A gift to be treasured. A gift I would take care not to lose. And if that really *was* a cocoon she was all wrapped up in . . . well, to me it was a *beautiful* cocoon.

I wouldn't have changed it for the world.

AS I SAID, ANITA THINKS I HAVE A LOT OF FREE time now with nothing to do, a little dig about how much time I spend with Sam Toselli. But I can't help that, can I? I'm Sam's self-appointed tutor. The other guys' as well: Jason, Gabriel, Tim, and Drew. It's been their habit to drop by and sit in on our lessons, after they'd served a pretty lengthy out-of-school suspension for their crimes at camp, and they're all benefiting from them. Even Roger-the-Sadist, Sam's physical therapist, is benefiting. He told me that whenever he has trouble sleeping, he pictures me demonstrating the solution to an algebraic equation, and soon he's nodding right off. No doubt the problem had been keeping him awake.

And I'm busy in other ways. It's April now, and what with spring in the air and a young man's fancy turning naturally to track-and-field events, I recently joined the relay team. It was Coach Caruso's idea, and I'm actually quite good. For some reason being chased by a bunch of stick-wielding guys seems to bring out the athlete in me.

But I'm going to make it up to Anita. I'm going to ask her to go to the spring dance coming up at school. Go *with me*—not just at the same time—because with the school year coming to a close and high school just around the bend, I have a sneaking suspicion that any day now her perfectly beautiful cocoon may release its butterfly, and when it does, well, I don't have to tell you, *George R. Clark plans to be right on the spot.*

And if you're wondering what became of my deep love for Allison Picone—my undying devotion that perished so many months ago on that fateful class camping trip—well, I'm happy to report it *stayed* dead. I've gotten to know Allison a lot better since then. She drops in on me often, under the guise of visiting Sam's sickbed, and after careful consideration I find that I draw only one conclusion about her now. Allison is weird. It's the giggle, chiefly. It drives me straight up the wall. I think that if she can't learn to control it, then she ought to have it surgically removed. But, of course, I would never say that.

Only a jerk would say that, right?